CAN'T HOLD ME DOWN

Also by Lyah B. LeFlore

The World Is Mine

THE COME UP
CAN'T HOLD ME DOWN

WRITTEN BY LYAH B. LEFLORE
ILLUSTRATED BY DL WARFIELD

SIMON PULSE | New York London Toronto Sydney

SIMON PULSE

An imprint of Simon & Schuster Children's Publishing Division
1230 Avenue of the Americas, New York, NY 10020
First Simon Pulse paperback edition June 2010
Text copyright © 2010 by Lyah B. LeFlore
Illustrations copyright © 2010 by Darrick "DL" Warfield
All rights reserved, including the right of reproduction in whole or in part in any form.
SIMON PULSE and colophon are registered trademarks of Simon & Schuster, Inc.
For information about special discounts for bulk purchases, please contact
Simon & Schuster Special Sales at 1-866-506-1949
or business@simonandschuster.com.
The Simon & Schuster Speakers Bureau can bring authors to your live event.
For more information or to book an event contact the Simon & Schuster Speakers Bureau
at 1-866-248-3049 or visit our website at www.simonspeakers.com.
Designed by Mike Rosamilia
The text of this book was set in Zapf Elliptical 711 BT.
Manufactured in the United States of America
2 4 6 8 10 9 7 5 3 1
Library of Congress Control Number 2009939611
ISBN 978-1-4169-7964-7

*For Noelle, Jullian, and Jordan for constantly
motivating me to write and create for your generation and the
generations to come. And for every young person with a dream,
keep believing and don't let anyone hold you down!*
—Lyah B. LeFlore

*As always, to Lisa, Kaylee, and Dakota
for holding me down*
—DL Warfield

Acknowledgments

Very special thanks to my agent, Amy Schiffman, and to my partner in crime and illustrator, DL Warfield. We're makin' history with this one!

To my editor, Emilia Rhodes, for taking over my "baby" and believing in the power of The Come Up.

To Cara Petrus, as always, for your valuable creative input. Special thanks to my amazing Simon Pulse/Simon & Schuster family for your support: Bethany Buck, Mara Anastas, Jennifer Klonsky, Lucille Rettino, Rob Goodman, and Venessa Williams.

And last but certainly not least, huge thanks to the Come Up models: Chase as Blue; Tyler as Collin; Jeremy as Tommy a.k.a. Whiteboy; Bijon as Jade; Christy as Mamie; Jordan as Trevaughn a.k.a. Young Tre; and our newest cast member, Corde, as Miles.

—Lyah B. LeFlore

CHAPTER ONE

BLUE

Yeah, I was out of touch
But it wasn't because I didn't know enough
—Gnarls Barkley, "Crazy"

"Blue? Blue!" My mom's high-pitched shouts were about as agonizing as fingernails scraping across a blackboard. "Blue, you'd better get up and open this door!" And then the pounding on the door came. "I know you hear me!" I buried my face in the pillow in an attempt to escape the annoying parental demands.

My thoughts were beating a hole in my head. In less than twenty-four hours I'd gone from feeling like I was on top of the world to being at the bottom. I'd thought sleep would make it all go away. Unfortunately, I just kept having the same nightmare about the party at Club Heat last night. In it everyone was dancing and having a good time, then right before my eyes, the club suddenly went up in flames, and then the crowd began shouting,

"Burn, Blue, burn!" That was the end of the dream. *Poof!* Blue Up Productions literally *blew* up.

"You've got about three seconds to open this door!" I pulled the pillow tighter over my ears. That only muffled her loud shouts. "And someone's on the phone for you!"

"I'm comin'! Just a minute," I groggily replied, sitting up and wiping the sand from my eyes. I checked the clock. It was seven a.m. I dragged myself out of bed.

"You must be crazy, boy, having me wait outside this door!" Mom ripped into me before I could get the door open good. She was fully dressed for church and wearing a pissed expression on her face. "Your father and I are going to early service," she snapped, shoving the cordless into my hand. "I hope whatever kept you out till four in the morning was worth it, because that may be the last time you see the outside world! You've got some serious explaining to do," she said, sucking her teeth.

"Based on the looks of things, is it safe to assume you're not going to church? Humph! Well, I don't care how tired you are, I want this room *and* my kitchen cleaned by the time I get back. And just a warning, your father is so furious, he doesn't even want to see your face. You'd better be glad it was me and not him banging on this door!" She rolled her eyes. "I mean, this place better be spotless when we get back!" She whipped around and stomped away, leaving me with a blank expression on my face.

My life had just been washed down the drain and now she

was sweatin' me. Whatever. I wasn't feelin' her, my pops, or anything either of them had to say. I looked down at the cordless phone dangling from my hand. For a moment, I contemplated pressing the off button. I was betting all kinds of heads, especially Mamie and Tre, had been blowin' my phone up about last night, but screw it. Even if I wanted to talk to anybody right then I couldn't. My phone was busted. Maybe them and the rest of the vultures out to pick apart my body had finally tracked me down at home.

"Hello?" I said flatly, putting the phone to my ear, flopping back down on my bed, and closing my eyes.

"Yes, this is Holy Cross Hospital. Is this Blue Reynolds?" an official-sounding voice asked.

"Errum, yeah, I mean yes," I said, clearing my throat. "Speaking." I sat up abruptly. "Who is this again?"

"Sir, as I said, I'm calling from Holy Cross Hospital. We received two numbers at which to contact you, and I tried reaching you on two, four, zero—"

"Yeah, yeah, that line is down right now," I said, cutting her off, glancing across the room at the pieces of my broken cell staring back at me. "What's this about?" I was slightly agitated.

"Mr. Reynolds, I'm calling at the request of Tommy James," she said. I was wide awake now, but couldn't figure out who the heck Tommy James was.

"Who?"

"Sir, he says he's a friend of yours. He's a patient here at the hospital." I was silent, still trying to figure out who she was talking about.

"Can you describe him?" I was stumped, rubbing my head. I felt a massive headache coming on. "I'm just not sure."

"Okay, he's six-one, Caucasian, and his arms are heavily tattooed. This is Blue Reynolds, right? He said you were the best person to call and that you'd know how to contact a Ms. Hernandez or a Mr. Collin Andrews—"

"Oh, snap! Yeah, you're talkin' about Whiteboy!" I said, cutting her off. My heart raced. "What happened?" I demanded.

"Sir, please calm down. There was an accident; he's pretty banged up. He was alert when he came in late last night, and was able to give us your phone numbers. The doctor performed surgery this morning on his jaw, and it was successful. Right now he's heavily sedated, resting, but it's been a very rough morning."

"What kind of accident?" I frantically questioned. My head felt like it was swelling as she went on to explain how he'd suffered some additional head trauma and a severely broken hand from some sort of a physical altercation. A flashback of the disastrous party at Club Heat popped into my head. I remember Whiteboy's shouting match with that fool Lopez vividly. Their argument had escalated and exploded into a full-fledged melee. I should've known the beef between Whiteboy and Lopez wasn't just going to go away. Something must've jumped off after they left the club.

My brain was moving faster than my hand as I scribbled down the information the nurse was giving me. I needed to tell Collin, but my Sidekick was busted, and I couldn't send him a text. I guessed I could call from the house phone, but since we weren't speaking, what would I say? I mean, I'd look like I was using Whiteboy being in the hospital as an excuse to call and apologize or something. Never that!

On second thought, maybe it was best I got to the hospital, made an assessment of what was going on with Whiteboy, and *then* dealt with Collin. I jumped into a pair of sweats and my sneaks as fast as I could and dashed out of the house like a madman. I screeched out the driveway and smashed the gas. I tried to keep myself cool on the short drive over to Holy Cross. All sorts of crazy thoughts were flying through my head about how Whiteboy was going to look, but I was worried the most about his hand, praying it wasn't the one he drew with.

When I reached the hospital I took a deep breath before making my way inside. I prepared for the worst. My heart pounded faster and faster with each step I took down the bright, stark hospital corridor. The lone nurse sitting at the ICU station directed me to Whiteboy's room. I took another deep breath and slowly walked in. I don't think of myself as typically having a weak stomach, but seeing Whiteboy unconscious with his face all wired up, hooked up to all the machines and IVs, kind of freaked me out. I sat down slowly on the chair next to his bed. The nurse ran down Whiteboy's condition.

"Is he going to make it?" I said, worried.

"We've got the best doctors here to take care of your friend. It's just going to take some time. I know everything looks a little scary."

"What are all the tubes for?"

"Those are giving him fluid and nutrients since he can't move his mouth because of the broken jaw." She pointed. "The other wires are to monitor his heart and blood pressure. I think he was most devastated by the damage to his hand. It was practically shattered."

"Yeah, yeah, he's an artist." I clasped my hands, putting them up to my mouth, trying to make sense out of all this.

"Along with the head trauma and a couple of broken ribs, the rest, thankfully, is just a bunch of minor bruises and cuts. Your friend's a tough one, that's for sure. We've got him on a pretty heavy stream of pain meds," she rattled off while checking his chart.

I felt awful looking at him all black and blue, and with all that wiring in his mouth. I bowed my head and said a silent prayer. When I looked up Whiteboy was trying to open his eyes. He motioned toward his right hand. I knew it was killing him to be like that. He lifted his left hand and pointed to the pen and paper that was sitting on the bedside table.

"Yo, Whiteboy, you've gotta rest, man," I said in a low voice.

He was adamant, insisting I give him the pen. "Yo, even in the hospital you're still a soldier." I chuckled, carefully handing him the pen and holding the pad of paper. He weakly scribbled *hand* on the page.

"I know, but don't worry about your hand. They have real good doctors here and they said they're gonna work real hard to fix it."

He pointed to the pen and paper again. I held it up like before and he scribbled *Collin*. I dealt with his hand being jacked up better than him asking about Collin. How was I going to answer him? I shook my head, trying to give him some reassurance that Collin would be there. Except, the truth was, I was lying.

I couldn't tell him that we weren't speaking, and that the stupid fight *he* got himself into at the club was the cause of everything being so messed up. Blue Up Productions, me, Collin, Jade, Rico Tate, Young Tre, Ill Mama, it was all a wrap! My career as a club promoter was finished! Grand opening, grand closing, in the blink of an eye. I was starting to get mad all over again just thinking about it.

"I'll tell him. Don't worry," I said, offering a reassuring smile. Whiteboy grimaced in pain before the meds took him back under. After a while, I must've drifted off too. I felt a light tap on my shoulder. I was being awakened by the nurse. She informed me that I'd have to leave the room so the doctor could examine Whiteboy. I looked at the clock and saw that I had been there for nearly an hour already. He was resting. It was a good time for a coffee break.

When I stepped off the elevator on the main floor, I immediately thought about Jade. I knew she wasn't checking for me right then, but I figured since Holy Cross is the biggest hospital in Silver Spring, perhaps there was a chance she was there with her mom.

"Excuse me, I'm trying to find out if a Ms. Donna Taylor is a patient here," I said, leaning against the information desk. A few moments later the silver-haired woman looked up and smiled.

"Yes, she's on the second floor. You can check in at the east nurses' station."

Yes! There is a God! I thought. A bolt of energy shot through my body. I quickly dashed into the gift shop across the hall and scooped up a bouquet of flowers. A million things ran through my head about Jade as I raced to the elevators. I pressed the up button. I just knew that when she saw me she'd race into my arms and all would be forgiven. We'd just had a dumb misunderstanding.

Even though I didn't know exactly what was wrong with her mom, I was sure Jade needed me right now. I *had* to be there for her. When the elevator doors opened, I froze. Mamie's text after the party suddenly flashed across my mind:

IT'S BEST YOU DON'T CALL BACK.

I stood there, stuck like a deer in headlights, trapped in quicksand.

"Son, are you getting on?" the lone elderly lady on the elevator asked. I shook my head no. Maybe it was best to leave it be. The doors closed. I dumped the flowers in a nearby wastebasket. Screw it! I've got my pride, too.

I felt even more defeated about the whole Jade situation by the time I got back to the ICU floor, where Whiteboy's room was. As I made my way down the hall toward his room, I could see him lying in his bed through the room's sliding glass door. I was suddenly smacked with guilt. Collin should be there. I owed it to him to tell him about Whiteboy being in the hospital. I had to put my anger aside.

Out of habit I reached for my cell to text him and was quickly reminded it was out of commission. One of the nurses directed me to a nearby phone. I was actually hoping Collin *wouldn't* answer. He probably wouldn't recognize the number anyway. I was prepared to leave a message and keep it movin'. I held my breath. After two rings Collin picked up.

"Hello?" I was shocked he'd actually answered the call. My words were momentarily trapped in my throat.

"Um, yo, it's me. Whiteboy's in ICU at Holy Cross," I said with short, direct words.

"I'm on my way," he said, quickly hanging up.

There, I had done it, but only for the sake of Whiteboy. I re-entered Whiteboy's room and plopped down in the chair next to his bed. I closed my eyes and let out a deep sigh. He was asleep. My stomach was beginning to knot up in anticipation of Collin's arrival. I put my face in my hands, reflecting on the party disaster again. I felt nauseous like Rabbit in *8 Mile*. I got up and rushed to the bathroom. I dry heaved a few times. False alarm.

I rinsed my face with cold water and stared at my pensive reflection in the mirror. I hit the light and exited the bathroom only to be greeted by a silent Collin standing in the doorway of the room. His chest was heaving as if he had sprinted all the way there. Collin slowly walked over to Whiteboy, who was asleep. He pulled up a chair and sat down. He didn't bother to speak, so I didn't either.

"What happened?" he asked with a clenched jaw, finally breaking the silence after several minutes.

"He was in a fight. They're worried about his head injuries, and his hand is basically destroyed. I'm thinkin' something went down with those cats he was beefin' with after the club," I said, shaking my head. "I don't know much else, except he drove himself to emergency."

"He's bad." Collin nodded.

"Real bad," I replied, putting my hand up to my mouth. "They said he'll probably be wired up at least four weeks."

"What else did they say about his hand?" he asked.

"He'll need surgery. I don't know what he's gonna do if he can't draw."

There was more silence. You could slice the tension in the air. It was all still too fresh. The only thing that kept flashing back to me were Collin's words from last night: *Maybe some things just aren't meant to be . . .* When your boy tells you something like that, you just don't shake it off that easily.

CHAPTER TWO

COLLIN

Papa isn't dumb, he understands what this means
His dream is my dream, my dream is his dream
—Asher Roth, "His Dream"

I stood across the street on Connecticut Avenue, staring at the large brass plate above the entrance to my father's office building. THE LAW OFFICES OF ANDREWS, WEINBERGER, AND TAUB was etched into it. Those words were a stark reminder of the fact that I needed to start accepting things and fast. It had to be my father's way or no way. Just like I'd already accepted that my friendship with Blue was pretty much nonexistent. That was evident at the hospital.

Sure, I was bummed about the party, more so about White-boy. That was really affecting me mentally. I felt guilty. I even regretted the fact that I'd had to walk away from Blue Up. I've never been one to just abandon my responsibilities, but to be honest, Blue was getting out of control. Here I was doing everything I could to be a loyal "partner." I'd never had a problem playing my role as the get-it-done-right-hand-guy. Blue was always the idea man. However, it's about mutual respect, and at a certain point the respect wasn't being reciprocated. He should've listened to me. You have to crawl before you can run! Now look at everything. We barely said ten words to each other during that whole time we were at the hospital visiting Whiteboy. It was like we were total strangers.

I probably shouldn't have been putting it all on him. I wasn't sure of what I wanted. My relationship with my father had always been a thorn in my side. I let myself be pushed in ways that worked for Blue's best interest instead of my own. Do I think it could've all been incredible one day? Sure, maybe? I don't know, with some time, I guess. But none of that mattered at this point. What mattered was that I was an Andrews, destined to follow in my grandfather's and father's footsteps. What mattered was getting out of high school holding the top spot in my class, and solidifying my place at Georgetown.

It was time to grind it out. I was going to use my dad's connects to pave the way, but I was going to make my own mark. To hell with yesterday! It's all about today, tomorrow, the next day, and beyond. No apology from Blue was big enough as far as I'm concerned. Blue *had* to do things his way. Too bad Whiteboy's hand was the sacrificial lamb.

Blue needed to know that he was wrong, but until he told

himself the truth, I couldn't be around him. The sad part was that that day probably wouldn't ever come. Some people are incapable of seeing their faults. I'd tried to have his back as a friend, and whenever he did something foul, I let it slide. I wouldn't cave in like the past anymore.

I blew out a puff of air and adjusted my shoulders, releasing the tension in my neck. I checked my watch. It was seven thirty a.m. and a glint from the early Monday morning sun bounced off the plaque in the wall. My necktie felt like it was cutting off my airflow. I had to look the part, dress the part. After all, I was an Andrews. With a hard swallow, I pushed down a dry lump stuck in my throat and made my way across the street. My grandfather built this law firm brick by brick. My father, the big-time lawyer and lobbyist, had taken it to stardom in the political arena, and it sat on prime Washington DC real estate, at Connecticut Avenue and K Street.

This was the playground for the powerful. The firm's pockets were lined with stacks of cash from representing some of the country's top pharmaceutical companies, fighting for the government's regulation of the banking industry, and representing a few defense contractors. This was my destiny and it was time I started facing that. Dad was right. Chasing pipe dreams with Blue was taking me nowhere. I checked my watch. It was time for me to turn a new page.

When I stepped off the elevator, the receptionist quickly pointed me toward the enclosed glass conference room. My father was running behind, due to a delayed international call. I scanned the pristine surroundings, as young hotshot lawyers with Capitol Hill dreams in their eyes moved with precision up and down the hallway and in and out of offices. The older lawyers moved slowly, sucking on the exhaust fumes of wealth. Lining the conference room's back wall was an impressive view of the National Monument.

Fifteen minutes later I was still waiting. On Mondays I didn't start class until nine. My dad insisted I stop by the office first. I couldn't believe that even with all his success, he still made it to the office every day by seven o'clock. I tapped my foot impatiently. I was going to hit crazy traffic on the way back to Silver Spring. What would normally be a fifteen- to twenty-minute drive was sure to take thirty to forty at this hour.

He was probably making me wait on purpose, applying slow, torturous pressure, before pouring salt on an open wound. So what that I had come crawling back on my hands and knees and with my tail tucked between my legs. Sometimes you have to swallow that jagged pill whole. I was about to give new meaning to the term "kiss ass."

My father finally entered the conference room. "Collin, there comes a time in every young man's life when he has to make decisions about his future," he said, standing in an authoritative glow. I stood up and shook his hand vigorously. "I'm glad that your little episode with your buddy Blue is over."

"Yeah, well, Blue and I aren't really hangin' out anymore," I said, sitting back down.

"I'm not surprised. I'm sure he had a lot of influence over you taking that money out of your account," he said, folding his arms across his chest. "You've always been easily swayed when it came to him."

"I wouldn't say all that. I mean, he took money out of his account, too."

"Not to be cliché, but two wrongs don't make a right decision. Look, I'm not interested in hearing anymore of this nonsense." He placed his palm on the conference room table and leaned toward me. "Son, I know you and Blue have known each other most of your lives, but sometimes the hardest thing people have to face is outgrowing each other. You're on a different path than the one he's on," he said, giving me a hearty pat on the back.

"I hope you learned your lesson after your recent behavior, taking money behind my back and skipping out on that important dinner. Professionalism and credibility is at the core of every great lawyer. An act of irresponsibility like that could've gotten your invitation to Georgetown's summer program revoked. Lucky for you, I have the kind of power I do." He chuckled. I nodded in agreement.

"Okay, on to more important topics, did you complete the assignment?" I nodded, reached into my backpack, pulled out a mahogany leather portfolio, and handed him a typed essay titled: "Making Smarter, More Practical Decisions."

"I'm sorry again, Dad. I'm really looking forward to hope-fully getting into the program. I promise I've got my priorities back in order." I sounded like a programmed robot, but I was going to make myself fall in line with my father's wishes even if it killed me.

"The summer program is going to be intense, and senior year will be here before you know it," he said, putting his hand on my shoulder. "I think you should spend your upcoming spring break interning around here—you know, shadowing one of our young associates. I'll have my secretary work some-thing out. In the meantime, I expect nothing less than straight A's for the rest of the year," he said, giving me another hearty pat, tossing the paper I'd stayed up all night writing into the garbage. I was seething with anger.

I'm sorry, didn't he know that I already had the highest grades in my class, or hadn't he even bothered looking at my last report card?

"By the time you get to Georgetown, you'll be leagues ahead of your classmates." He winked. "By the way, I'm going to reschedule that dinner with the president of Georgetown. I don't want to dwell on the past. You may not believe it, but I made my share of mistakes when I was your age too. See, son, I *do* believe in second chances." He winked again. My father had won. The prodigal son had returned and was under his control.

I quickly exited my father's office, then dashed out of

the elevator and raced toward my car, which was parked at the far end of the garage. I hit my car alarm remote. Just as I reached for the handle, my phone buzzed. It was a text from Mamie:

YO WHASSUP? LOOKIN' 4 U @ SCHOOL.
WHAT HAPPENED @THE PARTY?
ME & TRE NEED 2 HOLLA @ U AND BLUE???????????????

Brilliant! I thought, slamming my fist on the hood of the car. Now I had to deal with this crap. Handling Mamie and Tre was supposed to be Blue's job. He was supposed to tell them the deal. I quickly shot off a text:

CALL WITH BLUE. I'M DONE WITH BLUE UP

I pressed send and practically ripped the car door off getting inside. I yanked my tie loose and found myself gasping for breath. I was having an anxiety attack. I just wanted out of here. I tossed my phone in the backseat, turned the ignition, gunned the gas, and sped off.

CHAPTER THREE

BLUE

**Since the last time you heard from me I lost some friends
—Dr. Dre featuring Snoop Dogg, "Still D.R.E."**

I inconspicuously scrolled through my text messages while the last ten minutes of a film played in my history class. I'd just gotten a new freakin' phone and there were a gazillion messages waiting for me. Half of them were from Mamie and Tre, the other from Mischa, the random crazy chick who caused all the drama between me and Jade that night at the club. But one message in particular caught my attention right away. It was from Rico Tate. I cringed, taking a deep breath before opening it.

**HEADED 2 LA. B @ MY OFFICE NEXT MONDAY @ 7
NEED 2 DISCUSS THE PARTY – RT**

The other shoe had officially dropped and it was kicking me squarely in the butt. Rico giving me a week may as well have been an order to meet him today. Either way I was a dead man. In fact, I'd much rather have gotten it over with now. Why prolong the agony? So he could tell me how the club made a ridiculous amount of money off *my* party, but that I'd never see a dime of it?

I was still scanning my messages when I exited the classroom. I headed in the direction of the Cyber Café to grab a quick bite before my next class. Collin came around the corner. We made eye contact and it was like an enemy face-off.

"Yo, it's funny runnin' into you. I just got a text from Rico. He wants to discuss the damage at the club."

"So what?" he snapped.

"So are you planning on helpin' me out with this situation?"

"This is a joke, right? Am I on some wacked-out episode of *Punk'd*?" He snickered. "Un-freakin'-believable. I'm gonna be late for class." Then like a straight busta he turned and walked off in the other direction. *Yo, are you serious?* I thought. Dude straight tried to play me out. I bit my bottom lip to suppress my anger. I was so heated I couldn't get any words out.

I wanted to shout something ill at him or even better, body slam that fool, but it wasn't even worth risking suspension. I ain't got time for that bs. If that was how it was going down, cool, 'cause I knew when I dissed him next time, he was gonna feel it. No doubt!

Still buggin' out about my Collin encounter, I had to walk off my anger. I headed straight for the Cyber Café's sandwich bar and placed my order. I scanned the room. Jade crept into my thoughts. I was hoping I'd see her. No such luck. I spotted Mamie instead. She was going to hound me. I needed a quick exit plan, but not without my sandwich.

"Excuse me? Can you put a rush on that panini?" I impatiently asked the food service attendant. She gave me a look and twisted her mouth. Great, now she was going to take great joy in making me wait. She slowly removed my sandwich from the grill and took her sweet time sliding it across the counter to me. I quickly tossed money on the counter, snatched my food, and jetted toward the exit, pulling my baseball cap down on my head. I felt like I was on the run from those pesky TMZ cameras.

"Yo, Blue!" Mamie called out, racing toward me. I tried to do a fast break, like Collin's wack move, but she was already up on me, grabbing my shirt.

"Whassup? I've been callin' you like mad! What, I gotta show up at your house or somethin'? Whassup? What the hell is going on with all this MIA, cryptic message crap? Collin's supposed to be my boy and it took him forever to hit me back. When he finally did, he said something about you and him not dealing with each other anymore? That's some friggin' bullcrap!" She was talking a mile a minute without taking a breath.

"Mamie, chill! Now's not a good time," I said, attempting to push past her.

"Tell me about it! I think I can speak for both me and Tre—remember, your so-called artists! This is not the way you conduct business with your star talent!" she shouted, rolling her eyes.

"Look, it's complicated."

"I'm smart. I can figure it out. All I know is Tre and I rocked the house, and the party was off the hook. Unfortunately, due to your supreme wackness and inability to ward off the skeezers, I had to break up out of there with my girl. Then I get a text from Tre saying that some kind of fight broke out. What the hell is going on?" Mamie demanded.

"The party *was* great, but the fight that jumped off ruined everything. Once everybody scattered and the lights came up, the club was wrecked."

"Please excuse my lack of sensitivity, but that's the risk in the club game, right? Look, all we wanna know is when's the next joint? We wanna start working on some music together and a *real* show!"

"Mamie, it's done. I can't tell you when or *if* there'll be a next joint."

"Done? What's 'done' mean?"

"Blue Up's done! Me and Collin are done. And that fight at the club was between Whiteboy and some knuckleheads. Whiteboy ended up in the hospital. Now are you clear on what 'done' means?" I said, shaking my head. "I'm sorry, things weren't supposed to turn out like this."

"Yo, this is crazy! Back up. Is Whiteboy going to be okay? Does Collin know all this? I can't believe he didn't tell me," she said, pacing the floor.

"Yeah, he knows." I turned away.

"Hold up. Why are you acting like that?" I didn't respond. "What happened between you guys? Y'all are supposed to be boys, do or die!"

"Yeah, well, it's time for a change. All that's past tense. I thought he was going to be down for me for life just like I thought Jade would be there."

"No, let me break it down. My girl *was* there for you, but you tried to play her. Jade's a nice girl. She's not like all these other chickens around here. You might have them falling all over you, but that's not her get-down."

"I know it's not. That's why I fell so hard for her. I love her! Then I find out yesterday that her mom is in the same hospital as Whiteboy. I wanted to go see her, but she'd probably just have pushed me away."

"You're right about that!" Mamie rolled her eyes. "Blue, look, leave that situation with Jade alone, seriously. Jade is dealing with something way deep. I probably shouldn't tell you this, but her mom's cancer is back, and things aren't looking good."

"What? She never even told me her mother had cancer!" I said angrily.

"First of all, she's *my* best friend and I didn't know for a long time. So, see, it's not about me or you. It's not even about that chickenhead who was dancing all up on you at the party. She just needs her space."

"Can both of you give that a rest? Mamie, that was some random girl who goes to Bethesda – Chevy Chase and she rolled up on *me*! You know how some of these girls flow."

"I believe you, but my girl ain't used to stuff like that. Plus, put yourself in her situation. She comes back from getting some crazy news about her moms and you got some skeezer on you. I would bug out too. I got her back on this, Blue, and it's about respecting her wishes."

"But . . ."

"But nothing, dude! Look, take my advice and give Jade some time. She'll come around, hopefully. And as far as Blue Up, it's about the business. Y'all owe me and Tre. Whatever it is you're beefin' about, shut that crap down for real, dude," she said. "Maybe tensions are just high right now. You guys can bounce back from this."

"That ain't happening," I replied.

"This is so wack, Blue! Trey and I didn't take that attitude. We believed in you and Collin. We trusted you! Things finally started moving for me. There's more than just you and Collin's dreams at stake," she said, giving me a serious look. "Yo, figure it out! We need you guys to be back on point. We're all in this together."

"Look, the bottom line is that it's over. Pass that on to Tre, too. I'm sorry. I'm out!" As I walked away, her words sank deep. But honestly, I had bigger issues to face. I had to worry about what was going to happen when I saw Rico Tate.

CHAPTER FOUR

WHITEBOY

You said you a gansta but you neva popped nuttin'
You said you a wanksta and you need to stop frontin'
—50 Cent, "Wanksta"

"You're doing much better today. I have your pain medicine," the nurse said, injecting morphine into my IV.

I wanted to rip all these tubes out of my arms. Yeah, right, much better! My face felt like it had been split open with a machete, and my hand, like it had been smashed to pieces by a bag full of bricks. I thought things were supposed to get better as the days passed, but they weren't. Those nurses, doctors, the hospital, all of them were full of it. I wanted outta there!

I looked down at my hand, wrapped in layers of bandages. I tried like hell, but my fingers wouldn't move. My eyes rolled back. *Somebody help me! This can't be happening. I got nothin' if I ain't got my hand.* My heart pounded faster and faster. I tossed and turned. A gush of tears filled my eyes. The pain was too much. I moaned, unable to get any words out. They were caged in by the wires lacing my face and jaw. The pain exploded once again, this time in my head.

"You have to calm down, Tommy!" The nurse was doing her best to restrain me, but I started going into convulsions. She rang the red help button. "I need back up in B208, please!" she pleaded frantically into the call box.

"Hold him down" I heard another voice call out as several hands rushed in to restrain my body. I had lost control.

"He's going into shock. I'm upping his dosage," another voice said. Seconds later, a cool liquid seeped into my vein. My heart slowed. My breathing leveled off. I was fading.

"Tommy, can you hear us?" the first voice echoed in my head. My eyes were closed. The pain was subsiding. *Going . . . going . . . going . . . gone . . .*

I could see a bright light ahead, but I couln't reach it. Was that what death or almost death felt like? Damn, gangstas ain't supposed to go out like that. The pain was gone, but I was terrified. I only remembered feeling that scared one other time in my life. That was when my Grandma Rose was about to die. Fear ain't no joke.

I couldn't figure out how much time had gone by, but something strange was happening. It was like my body was frozen in this hospital bed, but my mind was still thinking and awake. I know that sounds totally bugged out, but even though my eyes were closed and I couldn't move, I didn't think I was dead. Does that make sense? Yo, maybe I'd slipped into the abyss or some crazy other world. In my insane dream state, it all started coming back to me—the club, Lopez, the fight, and how I ended up there . . .

Flash!

"Whassup, Whitebread!" Lopez smirked, purposely bumping me in the shoulder as he brushed past me in Club Heat's bathroom.

"Watch where you walkin', young!" I said, rinsing my hands as he headed into a nearby stall.

"What'd you say?" He stopped, looking over his shoulder at me.

"I said, you're rude and you need to learn some manners, young." I wiped my hands and exited the bathroom.

Flash!

"Ay, yo! Whitebread!" It was Lopez again. I was sick of this shit. "I see your punk-ass prep-school boys gave a tight little set." He sneered. "You still tryin' to protect your boy Rook? He said you had my money and now that fool done disappeared," he shouted across the dance floor.

"C'mon, Lopez, you know I don't have your money. I don't know nothin' about what you're talkin' about or you and Rook's business." I tried to shake this dude and continued dancing with a sexy Puerto Rican mami I'd been scoping out all night. I wasn't about to let him throw salt on my game. "Why don't you take your grimy-ass crew back to the gutta where you're more comfortable?"

"You know you got a smart-ass mouth. Like a bitch!" Lopez

smarted, pushing me from behind. I felt a surge of fury shoot through my body. I was sick of this fool poppin' off at the mouth, and before I could think, I had balled up my fists, turned around, and straight punched him in the face. I knew he had a crew, but I ain't no punk. I could take 'em all out if I had to. I had that fool in a headlock and his boys couldn't get through the crowded dance floor.

"Security! Security!" somebody shouted, as Lopez struggled for air. Girls were screaming, cats were running in every direction, chairs were flying, and glass was breaking. I hated that I had gotten into a fight at my boys' party, but sometimes you gotta do what you gotta do. I got in a few more punches and broke out.

Flash!

I was still chuckling to myself as I pulled up in front of Ms. Hernandez's house. I checked my reflection in the rearview mirror. Damn, I'd gotten the best of Lopez, but he had managed to get one good punch in. I dabbed the blood from a tiny scratch on my cheek, checked my face, got out, and hit my alarm.

High beams flashed behind me. It had to be my boys. I knew Blue and Collin were mad salty. I was prepared for them to flip out on me. I deserved it. I was in the wrong for fighting up in their joint. I got out the car and turned around.

"Turn them shitz off, yo!" The car's headlights were blinding me. I walked into the stream of light. "Yo, I'm sorry, guys. . . ."

Before I could get my sentence out, I was face-to-face with Lopez. He landed a serious left hook on my jaw.

Bam!

I stumbled to the ground. Then he landed another and another.

Bam . . . bam . . . bam!

Lopez and his crew straight jumped me. I tried to defend myself, but there were too many fists coming at me.

Bam! Bam! Bam!

Didn't he know I had a future to plan for?

Bam! Bam!

I was supposed to register for art school Monday morning.

Bam! Bam! Bam! Bam!

I had some good ideas I'd been sketching out. Don't hate on me 'cause I was tryin' to make something happen in my life.

Bam! Bam!

Lopez and his boys caught me off guard, but I was able to scramble to my feet. I stumbled backward and regrouped. Now he was gonna make me show him how I earned my rep. I rammed headfirst into his stomach, knocking him on his back. I proceeded to give him a first-class hood beat-down. That was until somebody hit me over the head with a bottle.

Craaack!

I was dazed momentarily. I fell to the ground and saw the sole of a Timberland coming toward my face. I tried to cover it with my right hand, but it was too late.

Craaack! Craaack! Craaack! Cruuunch!

It felt just like a Mack Truck had collided with my grill. I looked up one last time, directly into the barrel of a 9mm.

CHAPTER FIVE

BLUE

Doin' hundred fifty miles and runnin'
Get up in the way then you know that I'm gunnin'
—Rick Ross featuring Nas, "Usual Suspects"

I tapped my foot nervously, sitting on the basketball court bench outside Chuck Davis's rec center. Chuck was the one cat I could go to outside of my dad for help, and I *definitely* couldn't go to Pops on this situation. Chuck had become a mentor to me after hooking me up with Rico.

"Blue! My assistant said you were out here. You must be ready to start volunteering. So let's get you signed up. Our grand opening party is in a couple of months. I'm actually glad you stopped by. I might want to get that rapper kid of yours to perform at the party." His smile quickly faded when he saw the look on my face.

"Funny you should bring that up. That's sort of why I'm

here. I'm sure you're really busy, but I'm desperate. I need your help with something," I said, wringing my hands.

"What's up?"

"I'm in trouble with Rico Tate." He gave me one of those oh-no-not-again looks. "I'm sorry, but you're the only person I could go to for help."

"Okay, spill it," Chuck said.

"Well, um, see, I was on a good roll with him, but the last party I had turned out to be a disaster. There was a fight and the place got torn up. One of my homies even ended up in the hospital. Rico wants to meet in less than a week. I'll probably still owe him a grip. What do I do?"

"What does your partner, Collin, say?"

"That fool ran south. So I gotta handle my own now."

"Toss me the ball," Chuck said, shaking his head. I frowned, confused by how he was blowing me off.

"Huh?"

"I said pass the rock." I passed it to him. He set up his shot and *swish!* "I've only got time for a quick ten-point shoot-around. First one to reach ten wins. You win, I help you out with some advice one last time. I win, you *never* bother me with this Rico Tate stuff again, *and* you owe me some serious volunteer time here at the center. I'm already up two points."

"Okay!" I was desperate. I eagerly accepted his challenge, catching the rebound and passing him the ball again.

He dribbled then shot the ball. *Swish!* "Nothing but net,

baby! I never told you dealing with Rico would be easy. He didn't get to where he is without a helluva hustle and brain muscle." He caught his own rebound, went for the layup, and missed.

"What does that mean?" I grabbed the ball, dribbled, then shot. Missed by a mile. I was really off my game today.

"Rico isn't some run-of-the-mill street gangsta or hood," he said, shooting. "That's six-zero! Did you know he has an MBA from Harvard? He's no joke." He shot the ball again. It bounced off the rim. I caught his rebound and shot a smooth left hook. "Nice skills!" he said, stealing the ball and running it in for a sweet dunk. "Eight to your two!" he called out. "He's from the hood right here in southeast DC. So you've gotta be smart in your dealings." He dribbled.

"Chuck, I've been pretty dumb so far. I've lost my girl, and my dreams of having my own company are over. I've even severed ties with my boy, who's really like my brother. I got nothing else to lose, but more than anything, I can't afford *not* to be smart from here on out," I said, keeping my eye on the ball.

"First of all, you can't let minor setbacks shut you down. You have your whole life ahead of you," he said matter-of-factly. "I thought you were tougher than that, young bro. That's why I stepped out and gave you a good word." He pulled a fake move, pivoted, then took a shot. *Swish!* "Final point!"

"I thought I was too, and I appreciate everything you've done," I said, trying to catch my breath.

"Old school wins by a sweep!" he said, doing his version of a victory dance. We both laughed. "You know I'm gonna hold you to your volunteer work here, but I'm feeling generous today so I'm going to give you that advice anyway. The best way to even a score with Rico is to be honest, be humble. What are you, seventeen?"

"I'll be eighteen in six months!" I proudly boasted.

"Whatever, young bro. You've got real potential and natural ability, but do you know what your best asset is?"

I was baffled. "Bro, I'm lost."

"Whether you're seventeen, eighteen, twenty-eight, or fifty-eight. Your best asset is *you*. You're going to have to be willing to put in some work on this. Be creative. Use your head and come correct. You can't get through school without putting in the work. Life is the same way. Rico saw right through that big baller act you put on.

"He put you down not just because I introduced you to him but because he saw *your* potential earning power. Think about it. Would he really still be talking to you if you were finished? And sometimes you've gotta be that lone soldier, feel me?" What Chuck was saying was really starting to hit home. "That's enough free advice for the day. I'm going to start charging you soon!"

"You might have to put it on my tab." I let out an exasperated sigh.

"Grab that basketball and follow me inside," he said,

shaking his head. "I need you to set up some chairs for the after-school tutoring program that's already under way."

"Right now? Um, I thought the whole volunteer payback thing could wait a few days." I was hedging, searching for an excuse.

"Nah, young bro, I always collect my debts at the time they're due. But today I won't be too hard on you. However, you've gotta give me one night a week." He extended his fist.

"Bet!" I gave a big Kool-Aid smile, holding my fist out and tapping it against his. I quickly gathered my backpack, picked up the ball, and trotted off after him. Unfortunately, I knew that another set of issues, as in the parental kind, awaited me at home. Somehow I wasn't so sure it would go as smoothly with my dad as it had just gone with Chuck.

At home I'd been on edge since the morning after the party. My dad still hadn't had the so-called talk my mother told me to be expecting. I think Whiteboy being in the hospital had actually saved me so far. Maybe my dad felt a little sorry for what I'd been going through with that. Whatever the case, it was all good. Pops's wrath could be wicked, and for now I just needed to be focused on what I was going to say to Rico Tate.

For the second night in a row, me, my dad, and my mom sat in silence at the dinner table. Tonight there were two rules to keep in mind: Eat fast and avoid all eye contact. I shoved a forkful of meatloaf in my mouth, chasing it with a big gulp of iced tea. The sooner this meal was over, the better. I finished eating and pushed back from the table.

"May I be excused?" I asked.

"Hell no!" My dad shouted, slamming his water glass down on the table. "It's time to deal with this nonsense once and for all!"

"David, calm down," Mom added.

"I've been too damn calm, Carol. No more bs'ing. In the end he's only hurting himself and his future," he snapped, turning back to me. "Blue, I want an explanation about that party you had." His booming voice bounced off the walls. "And don't lie. You've done enough of that!" He was fuming. "Tell me the truth right now about that party you had!"

It was like I heard the voice of God or something. I took a deep breath. I had to man up and put on my game face. Sometimes it's about rollin' with whatever comes your way. I was seeing that a lot lately. I took another deep breath. "Well, see, the party started off great, but it got a little out of control and the club got damaged."

"No, Blue, you came into this house in the wee hours of the morning, violated the rules of this house, and furthermore violated our trust. I got a call from Collin's dad this evening, telling me that you and Collin apparently aren't friends anymore and that Collin took money out of his account to pay for that party you guys had. He suggested I check your account too. So I did, and guess what? I saw that there was money missing." I was cold busted, and to make it worse, that snitch Collin played me out.

"So now are you ready to tell the real truth?" He pounded his fist on the dining table.

"Okay, Dad, see, I can explain." I was sweating bullets.

"Then get to doing it!" he said, folding his arms.

"Well, I'm on to something big with this party thing. You always talk about investing in yourself first, and I took the money to get my company started. Collin and I were partners."

"Partners!" he shouted furiously.

"Well, the parties were going to lead to us building an entertainment empire. Unfortunately, the party got shut down. Now I'm probably going to owe the owner."

"I've heard enough. I should've known when you were doing all that talk about rappers and nonsense that you were up to something different than what I agreed to. I said I was fine with you giving these little parties here or there, not trying to make parties a career! Well, we've got some new rules around here. I want to see some grades, young man, you've got SATs to prepare for, and this summer you will get a job, and every penny you make will repay your college fund for that little personal investment you made. And the car is to be used only for necessity. No parties, no clubs, none of that nonsense."

"What do I do if I end up owing the club more money?"

"I don't give a damn. You're on your own. My problem is making sure you follow the rules in my house and that you do your best in school. I checked with your counselor at school, and as I suspected, you're doing just enough to get by in school. That's not acceptable!" He slammed his fist on the table again.

"I keep talking to you about college, but at this rate you may never make it to college. No son of mine is going to be a failure! You'd better get serious about high school. Three generations of college-educated Reynoldses in this family!" he warned. "For the rest of this semester, starting today, I want to see a change. Next year is crucial. If you don't get into college, you'll be on your own! And by the way, you're grounded indefinitely!"

"Grounded, but—"

"I'm done playing games with you, Blue. You don't have it like your rich buddy Collin!" he said, standing up, throwing his napkin on the table. "School, library, and home—that's it!" He began pacing the floor.

"What about seeing my friend in the hospital? Also, Chuck asked me to volunteer at the rec center after school."

"I'll *think* about the rec center. As far as the hospital, I realize it's your buddy, but you've got to get your priorities together. You can go visit him on a limited basis, but I wanna see some progress first. You understand?" he demanded. I nodded eagerly.

"And make sure you leave your set of car keys here. You'd better get real familiar with the Metro or walking!" he stormed off and slammed his bedroom door, punctuating the severity of his words.

When the coast was clear I made my way upstairs to the

bathroom. I turned on the hot water and inhaled the steam, still shaken up from my dad's explosion. I needed a plan for sure this time. I had to make sure I got back in with Rico. My dad would never understand just how powerful Rico Tate was.

The countdown to my face-off with Rico had begun. The way I saw it, I had two options . . . sink or swim. It was time to start swimming like hell. I might have to fight the current going upstream, but I didn't have a choice. By any means necessary, and that was real!

CHAPTER SIX

JADE

I'm so over it, I've been there and back
—Kristina DeBarge, "Goodbye"

Last period ended and I rushed to collect my things. Today was the first official meeting my biology teacher, Mr. Owens, was holding for the students he had hand selected to compete for a slot in the High Schoolers for Medicine program, or HS4Med, at Howard University, which was held annually during spring break. It was normally just open to seniors, but based on my GPA, I was an exception. I was going to surprise my mother after the initial meeting.

I was so nervous walking into the biology lab. There were students gathered who I'd never seen. It was like an SSH brainiac fest.

"Miss Taylor, just the person I've been waiting for." Mr. Owens's warm greeting took the edge off. He was a robust white-haired man who sort of reminded me of an Albert Einstein. He had that mad-scientist vibe, but he was my favorite teacher at SSH. There was a preppy but fly-dressed guy standing next to him. "I'd like for you to meet Carlos Reyes," he said. "Carlos, this is Jade."

"I've heard a lot about you," Carlos said as he extended his hand. I was taken aback by his comment and somewhat overpowered by the charm that oozed from his smile. It didn't hurt that he was gorgeous, too. His skin looked like a creamy cup of café au lait.

OMG, and the dreamiest eyes I'd seen in a long time. Well, not as dreamy as Blue's, but that would be hard to beat. Blue had the kind of eyes that sucked you in, made you want to fall in love. But I needed to get rid of any thoughts of Blue.

"Um, usually a person reciprocates the gesture." He chuckled, still holding his hand out.

"Oh, my bad," I apologized, quickly sticking out my hand. "So what, um, have you heard? I hope all good," I replied coyly.

"Definitely. Your application was really good. I hear you'll probably make a great doctor one day." I was about to respond to his flirty comment, but Mr. Owens interrupted our subtle connecting moment.

"Jade, I'd like for you to sit in the front row. We're about to start." I anxiously took my seat. There were about ten of us gathered. "Welcome, everyone," Mr. Owens announced. "You are here because you are the finalists for a very unique program we've set up with Howard University for minority students interested in the medical field. Your grades are outstanding, but only five of you can be chosen after you turn in your final essay. Those attending the program will be mentored by a current pre-med student at Howard.

"Carlos is an honors student in the pre-med program, and one of the mentors. Stay tuned for the date of the next meeting, when the winners will be announced. In the meantime, please leave your contact information on Mr. Reyes's sheet," Mr. Owens announced before excusing us.

I checked my phone. I wasn't going to miss this meeting for the world, but I couldn't be late for work either. My boss Miss Shante was a stickler for time. Plus, I was working only half a shift so I could make it to the hospital to see my mom later. Thank God Mamie had agreed to cover the rest of my hours tonight.

I jumped two people in line, pissing them off, but whatever, I had a job to get to. I could feel the weight of Carlos's eyes on me as I scribbled my e-mail address and phone number down on the sheet. I swallowed a major blush, quickly regrouping. I gave a quick but cute good-bye and rushed out.

By the time my shift ended, I was beat. I exhaustedly slid an iced latte in front of Mamie, then removed my apron and pulled up a chair to join her and sipped on a cup of hot ginger tea.

"I am so glad Miss Shante let you cover my last hour and a half," I said.

"He's a bug-out, right? Oops, I mean *she's* a bug-out!" We snickered. Today Miss Shante donned what looked to be an outfit paying tribute to Rihanna, complete with the fly short, asymmetrical haircut. She was sitting at a nearby table, working on next week's schedule. *She* cut her eyes in our direction at our giggly outburst.

"Girl, I've got some serious studying to do after I go check on my mom," I said, taking another sip.

"No problema, mamacita. What do I need to hurry home to my aunt for? Anything for you."

"God, I'm beat. I hope I make it to the hospital before she goes to sleep. We always say our prayers together at night."

"Aw, how sweet."

"We've been doing it like forever." I smiled.

"She doing any better? I've been praying for her," she said, sipping from her drink.

"Thanks girl, a little bit. I'm just trying to be strong for her. I'm praying her cancer will go back into remission."

"It will." Mamie grabbed my hand and squeezed it tight.

"It's so tough. I just figure if I kick butt in school, I can make her so proud she won't even think about being sick."

"Dang, girlie, can you get any higher than an A?" Mamie teased.

"Hey, school is my escape, like music is yours. When you've been through what we've been through with her sickness, you learn to lean on positivity. Speaking of positivity, I do have a little bit of good news. I'm one of the finalists for this summer program at Howard's medical school for high school students interested in studying pre-med in college. And you know Howard's like my number one choice."

"What! You'd better work it, mami! I'm so proud of you!" Mamie screeched loudly, throwing her arms around me.

"Hold up, I'm not *in* yet. I'm kinda nervous. I have to write this killer essay. The competition is serious. But the kinda cool thing is that they have current HU students as the mentors. One of them was there today. He was totally hot," I gushed.

"What! You are really over Blue, huh?"

"Girl, stop buggin', I'm just admiring. First of all, the Blue drama may have ruined it for the next ten guys! Carlos is in college. You know he would not be checkin' for no high school junior!"

"Oooh, a college man! How exciting. See if he has friends!" We slapped high fives.

"Nah, it's all business. I'm not messing up this opportunity."

"Chick, you have this so aced in the hole!"

"I sure hope so." I bit my bottom lip. I only wished I had as much confidence in myself as Mamie had in me. "Getting in would be a huge blessing. I just hope I can keep my head together to get through the process. I feel super stressed. Plus, the timing of all this crap with Blue doesn't help. What a freakin' disappointment." I shook my head in disgust.

"Jade, maybe you're being too hard on a brotha."

"Are you serious?" I said, rolling my eyes. "Blue may have been a cutie pie and had crazy charm, but he wasn't genuine, you know? I went against what I promised myself, and that was to focus on school and worry about a relationship when I got to college." A flash of anger came over me just thinking about the time I wasted falling for Blue's bs.

"I don't know if I agree about the genuine part. Sure, he may have an ego out of this world, but as much as I hate to say it, that dude cares about you. I know that. I saw it in his eyes." I looked at her with an attitude and rolled my eyes again. "Listen, I don't want you to be mad, but I have a confession to make," Mamie said, nervously biting her bottom lip. "Okay, well." she took a deep breath. "I told Blue your mom has cancer and he's really worried." Mamie flinched as if her own words had smacked her in the face.

"Mae, why? Urgh! If I wanted him to know, I would've told him!" I said with a huff, rolling my eyes and folding my arms across my chest.

"I'm sorry, but he says he loves you, girl. Anyway, he's actually dealing with a lot too. He and Collin aren't friends anymore, and Whiteboy got into a horrible fight after the party and has been in the hospital—coincidentally, Holy Cross. You've had so much on you with your mom and all, and I didn't want to give you more bad news."

"Hold up, Whiteboy's in the hospital? That's terrible." I frowned.

"Yeah, Blue said he's really messed up. And the fact that Blue and Collin are on the outs is even more messed up at a time like this."

"Yeah, it is, but on the real, Mae, I can't get caught up in that emotional stuff," I said, turning up one corner of my mouth. "I'm sorry, but I just don't want to really hear Blue's name or anything about him." I shook my head, sipping from my cup.

"So hold up. I know you're mad at him, but don't you care about him and Collin?"

"Not really. It ain't my business. Can we just *please* drop talking about them?"

"Okay, okay. And you promise you don't hate me for opening my big fat mouth?"

"No, I don't hate you, but the next time you do something like that, be expecting a beat-down!" I playfully shoved her.

"Good! I can live with a beat-down, just don't touch the face. That's my moneymaker!" We shared a laugh. "On an upbeat note, I did a set last night at the club. Some record industry people were in the house. I didn't get home until two a.m. The party was crazy! I even got some business cards so that I can send some folks my demo. Girl, I need some major sleep."

As Mamie rambled, thoughts of Blue seeped into my head. Truthfully, I did kinda feel bad about him and Collin. I didn't know what happened between them, but I was sure he was upset. They were as close as brothers.

"I swear, Jade, when I'm spinning, I lose track of time. I know

I've got the goods with my music, and I'm feeling a sense of urgency now more than ever." Mamie was yapping like some kind of windup toy. "That's why I've gotta figure out my next moves," she said, tapping her nails on the table. "What do you think?" Mamie snapped her fingers in front of my face. "Um, hello!"

"Huh?" I said, popping back into reality.

"Girlie, whassup with you? It's like you're in some far-off zone. Awww, you're thinking about Blue, aren't you?" she teased.

"Don't even play yourself saying stuff like that. Blue is the last thing on my mind," I said, checking my watch. "Anyway, look, I gotta go."

"Well, how about I just blow this place off and give you a ride to the hospital?"

"No, girl. You need to make *all* your money. The Metro lets me off right in front, and I'm going to catch a cab home from there. My mom made me promise."

"Okay, but hit me when you get home so I know you made it safely." We gave each other a big hug. I felt myself getting emotional as tears welled up in my eyes.

"Jade, are you about to cry?" Mamie probed, pulling back and looking at me. "I'm so going with you!"

"No, I'm cool, really. It just hits me like that sometimes. God, my mom's such a fighter, Mamie," I said, wiping my eyes. "I'm usually pretty good at keeping things to myself, but I couldn't help it, I guess."

"Girl, that's what I'm here for."

"I don't know if I could be as strong as she is if I were in this situation, Mae." I wiped my eyes again. "I just feel like it's so unfair." I stood up and grabbed my oversize tote. "Anyway, I'm good. I need to make it there before visiting hours are done." We hugged once more and I jetted.

Unfortunately, the Metro was running late, and when I walked into her room, my mom was peacefully sleeping. I smiled to myself. Careful not to wake her, I quietly walked over to her and kissed her on the forehead. I guessed I'd have to save my news about the program at Howard for another day. I decided to write her a note. *YOU'RE MY HERO, LOVE JADE.* I slipped it under her pillow and kissed her again before tiptoeing out of the room.

I was dog tired and could barely keep my eyes open on the taxi ride home but had to dig up enough energy to finish my AP Biology paper. I was hoping I'd get a chance to start on that essay for Howard, but that would have to wait. However, I perked up immediately when the driver pulled in front of my apartment building and I saw Blue standing on the sidewalk holding a bouquet of flowers.

"Hey, Jade," he called out as I paid the cabdriver and exited the taxi.

"Blue, what do you want?" I said, rolling my eyes.

"I didn't come to bother you. I just wanted to let you know

that I was thinking about you and that I'm here for you." He handed me the flowers. Now I *was* mad at Mamie for telling him about my mom.

"These are nice, but you didn't have to," I said politely, refusing to take them.

"I wanted to." He offered them again.

"Blue, I really appreciate the gesture, but I've gotta get in the house."

"Okay, but can we at least talk about what happened at the party?"

"I'm not mad about that anymore, and I'm too tired to argue, Blue."

"I don't want to argue. I'm on the outs with my pops. Me and Collin aren't homies anymore. My other boy is messed up in the hospital. Having you in my life would at least make things better, give me some hope. I just want another chance."

"Another chance at what? Blue, it's over. Hey, I'm really sorry about all the crap going on in your life, but trying to come at me ain't the answer. I'm focused on school and my mom. That's all that matters."

"I understand. So, I'll back off." He paused. "Just tell me why you didn't tell me about her illness."

"I don't know. I guess I'm just private like that," I stressed.

"Okay, I can respect that, but this is me. I wanna be in your life, and I need you in mine. I need you on my team, J." He was starting to beg, and begging was not sexy at this point.

"Blue, I feel for you, but the reality is that some people are dealing with life-or-death issues. I'm not really interested in Team Blue." There was an awkward pause. "I don't need a lot of rah-rah in my life. I gotta go. And can you do something for me?"

"Anything."

"Can you just leave me alone?"

"Jade, I love you," he said, handing me the flowers one last time. I let out a frustrated sigh and took them.

"Love? What the hell do you know about love, Blue?"

"I know it's about two people being there for each other. I need you, Jade. I thought you loved me too."

"God, you're so selfish! It's not always about *you*, Blue Reynolds!" I said in disgust. "Look, I thought I loved you too." I pushed past him and made my way up the steps. "Some things just aren't meant to be. It was cool while it lasted, but I've gotta keep it movin'." I disappeared inside my building and didn't turn back. I was afraid I'd start crying if I did.

CHAPTER SEVEN

BLUE

Lemme put you on the game
—The Game, "Put You on the Game"

I made it onto the Metro just as the doors were closing. There wasn't an empty seat in sight. Thankfully, I just had three short stops to the hospital. I told my dad that I didn't start working with Chuck at the rec center until next week, from five till nine in the evenings. That was going to be my excuse to get out of the house for my meeting with Rico.

I slid to the back of the train, put my headphones on, and pressed play on my iPod. The music gave me a chance to think. Jade cutting me off was the final blow, and now it was all about readjusting my game. Maybe rollin' solo was what I had to do to take it to the next level. I even shut down tweeting, checking my messages, and getting caught up in the Facebook hype.

Too much fallout gossip and talk about the party was still going on. Unfortunately, I was digging as deep as I could, but still not coming up with much in terms of what my angle with Rico Tate was going to be.

The Metro screeched to a stop, and I made a mad dash off the train, finally able to breathe again. I exited the Metro station and jogged a short block to the hospital. Pops made me put off coming here for a few days because I had to, as he called it, "get my school priorities straight." He had no idea, but I still couldn't focus on schoolwork. All that was on my brain was that money I was going to owe Rico. But thank God for the get-out-of-jail pass for the library and the hospital my dad gave up, or I was going to go stir-crazy.

I only hoped Collin had already come and gone. Seeing him today might have made me totally flip. We'd been avoiding each other at school. I was glad we don't have any classes together. I still couldn't believe he told his father about the money I took out of my account. That was a major snitch move. Oh, but don't trip, in due time I'd confront him. Pleeze believe it!

I hopped off the elevator on Whiteboy's floor, and who was standing outside his room in the hallway but Collin's punk ass in the flesh. I swallowed my repugnance. *Just try to play it cool and keep your distance*, I told myself. Honestly, I felt like punching him in the face, but I knew I had to be bigger than him. I was there to see *my* boy, pay my respects, simple as that. Hopefully, he was leaving anyway.

I saw the nurse walk over to Collin and tell him something. Whatever it was must've been pretty disturbing, because he pounded his fist into his hand, then covered his mouth. He looked like his legs were going to give. The nurse gave him a consoling pat on the shoulder.

"Nurse, what's up? What happened?" I said, rushing over to where they were standing.

"Your friend can explain, but I'm sorry, Tommy slipped into a coma."

"Hold up! Why didn't the hospital call?"

"They *did* two days ago. I guess you never checked your messages," Collin said in disgust. "I just happened to stop by after the library."

"Gentlemen, I realize this can be very stressful," she said, sensing the division between us. "But remember it's about the patient. Your friend suffered a great deal of trauma and quite a lot of shock. We're monitoring him at this point. I'm sorry, but I've got to get to another patient. I'll be around to answer any further questions." She walked away.

I pulled out my phone and saw that my voice mail alert was flashing. "Urgh!" I said, slamming my phone shut. I felt like an idiot. I tried feverishly to explain: "I'm sorry. I've just been really busy. I haven't checked my messages."

"Whatever, dude, I gave them my number for the next time. Hopefully, there won't be one." Collin cut his eyes at me. I had to use all the restraint I had in me not to hit him. My nostrils flared. One more comment and I was gonna floor his ass.

I quickly charged past Collin into Whiteboy's room and made my way over to his bed. Collin followed. But the moment I looked at Whiteboy lying there with his eyes closed, I quickly forgot about my beef with Collin. I didn't even realize he had been standing next to me for several minutes. Collin and I were both speechless and solemnly looking down at him. The whole scene was surreal.

"I can't look at him like this. It's our fault," Collin snapped, abruptly turning and walking back out of the room. I quickly followed him.

"Yo, hold up, C!" I called out, catching him as he stepped onto the elevator. He furiously pressed the P1 button. "What do you mean it's *our* fault? That's bullcrap! Whiteboy got himself in that fight!" I shouted.

"Yeah, and where did that fight happen? Our party! That friggin' party caused all this fallout," he retorted.

"Yo, you're delusional. Those cats had it in for Whiteboy, party or no party!"

"All I can say is that he's in a coma now. Maybe your conscience is clear, but mine isn't!" The elevator doors opened, and Collin stormed off.

"Yo, my conscience is very clear!" I said, racing after him.

"Why am I not surprised?" he sarcastically replied, stopping and turning to face me. "The way you act says a lot about your definition of friendship."

"Friendship?" I laughed. "You're comedy, homie. I told you Whiteboy having beef with those dudes had nothing to do with me. I mean, I'm just as sorry as you are about things, but you're blowing this way outta proportion." By this time we'd made it to where we were both parked. "But I'll tell you one thing, what this whole thing does do is says a lot about the definition of *bitchassness*! Snitches know what that is real well, don't they?" I said, ripping into him. I couldn't hold it any longer.

"What the hell are you talkin' about?" Collin shouted back.

"I'm talkin' about you pullin' that bitchass move and telling your dad about the money I took from my savings account." We faced each other in an intense showdown.

"F you! I was loyal, and I risked my future for your crap!"

"No, playa, loyal would be helping me get Rico Tate off my ass. I like how you never answered me the other day when I told you I had to deal with the fallout from the party. Must be nice to walk away from obligations, your word, deals, you know what I mean," I chided.

"You just can't leave it alone, can you? Does Whiteboy have to die for you to realize? I told you some things just aren't meant to be. Look, I want no part of Blue Up or Rico Tate—none of it! You're the genius, fix it or, better yet, manipulate him like you did me!" he shouted, shoving me in my chest.

"Yo, for real, you need to break yourself, C," I warned, grabbing him by the collar and slamming him against his car. "And you need to quit whining and being a punk! You're lucky I don't kick yo ass for pullin' this crap! You owe me!"

"Get the hell off me! I don't owe you anything! You're on your own." Collin broke free from my grasp and angrily hit the button on his remote to unlock his car door.

"What about your word being your bond?" I shouted. "You can be out, but just remember that if all this crap hadn't gone down, you would've been right there with me, splittin' the cash. You want what's convenient for you, C!" I said, throwing my arms in the air.

"Oh, damn, that's a concept! I guess selfishness is contagious, right, Blue? Except when you need someone to execute the work."

"Execute? You're an f-ing joke. Remember Blue Up was *my* vision. I got shit jumpin' off, young, and I can do it again. I can make it hot for real next time. Dolo!" Our shouts must've alerted a nearby security guard combing the parking lot in a golf cart. He slowly rolled past us and gave us a look.

"Is everything all right, gentlemen?" the security guard asked. "You know this is hospital property. Either keep it down or leave! Thank you!" He nodded before pulling off.

"I'm out! I've got an important *meeting* to get ready for tomorrow!" I lowered my voice, but purposely emphasized the word "meeting."

"I'll make sure to tell Whiteboy *if* he ever wakes up!" Collin slammed his door, started his engine, and zoomed off.

"Yeah, you do that and keep runnin', C!" I shouted. Damn! It was like the hole kept getting deeper and deeper. Collin proved he was the weakest link. I had to be about gettin' mine. The game had officially changed! That's whassup.

CHAPTER EIGHT

MAMIE

I like that boom boom pow
Them chickens jackin' my style
—Black Eyed Peas, "Boom Boom Pow"

Mr. Jones, the school counselor, was rattling on and on about how I was technically on probation and that I should consider myself warned.

Blah, blah, blah . . .

"Ms. Frazier, we've notified your aunt. She was very concerned about your poor attendance record and the fact that you haven't been turning in your assignments on time. You may be required to do summer school and, if things don't improve, possibly finish a semester to a year later than your class. There are options," he said, clearing his throat, "but you'll have to meet us halfway."

I watched his lips moving in sync with an imaginary beat.

I had just burned a CD of this crazy beat I wanted to turn into a track for Tre. I pictured myself tapping it out on my beat machine. *Boom tat boom tat.* Then how I added some scratching and mixing, working up a sweat on the ones and twos.

Awicka wicka wicka.

I was in another world, and so not trying to hear any of this.

Boom boom pow . . . freshhhhhh!

"Ms. Frazier, I hope we don't have to have this conversation again."

"No, Mr. Jones, I understand and I'm very clear." I smiled politely, gathered my purse and books, all of which had quietly collected dust over the past several weeks, and exited. All I could think about was that hot-to-death beat in my head. Poor guy, he didn't even realize that I had more important things on my mind, like hooking back up with Tre and making some dope music.

The beat I had created was giving my brain a major workout. I was excited just thinking about how insane Tre was going to sound when I finished this track for him to spit on. In the meantime I had to get him a copy of some tracks I had been working on. I shot him off a quick text.

WHERE U AT?

THE CRIZZO

LEAVING SCHOOL NOW GOTTA DROP SOME HOTNESS OFF

Perfect timing! Tre was walking up his front steps when I pulled up. He looked like he had just arrived. "I couldn't wait! I got some insane new beats for you, baby, baby," I said, exiting the car, pulling a CD out of my purse, and waving it in the air.

"Whassup, ma?" Tre said, giving me a delicious hug. "You got that fire?"

"Bam!" I said, handing it over to him. "I just burned these beats off my computer."

"I've been writing a lot of new stuff. So this is great."

Just then a cutie in cornrows burst out the front door.

"What's poppin', cuz? Show me some love!" he said, making a grand entrance and flashing a thousand-watt smile accented by sexy dimples.

"Oh, snap!" Tre's eyes went wide. They gave each other a series of pounds and brotherly hugs. "What are you doin' here?"

"I came to kick it with you for a minute. You know moms be trippin', but I'll get at you later about all that," he said.

"Those sneaks are fly." Tre pointed to his shoes. "You know you always be rockin' that cool Calistyle."

"Aw, you like these, huh? Just a li'l somethin' somethin'." He broke out in the old-school gangsta two-step. We all laughed.

"I haven't seen you in a minute, fool! What it do!" The cutie beamed.

"Errum!" I cleared my throat loudly. "A formal introduction would be nice," I interrupted.

"My bad. Mamie, this is my cousin Miles from Cali," Tre proudly announced as Miles slid between us.

"Oh, you know I would never dis the ladies," he said, showing me that scrumptious smile again, then he lifted my hand and gently kissed it. "Whassup, boo." Miles beamed. Miles's gear was tight too, from his cool Ed Hardy T-shirt and jeans to some fly Chuck Taylors.

Tre was somewhat taken aback. "C'mon with that corniness. 'Whassup, boo,'" he imitated.

"I don't know, I kinda like it. By the way, nice hand," I said. Miles's hands were strong yet gentle, but not in a girlie way.

"That's my prize hand. How I be catchin' them passes and runnin' them touchdowns," Miles bragged.

"Oh, for real? I'mma have to check out your game sometime," I coyly replied.

"Fo sho, boo, I bring the fire on and off the field."

"Yo, chill on all that weak rap. That might be how y'all do it in Cali, but that's played out around here, cuz," Tre said, twisting his mouth, making a slight dig. Miles gave Tre a playful shove. Hmmm, was my boy Tre getting jealous?

"Let me find out you hatin', Tre," I flirtatiously teased.

"Anyway, back to the music," Tre said, sitting on the steps and examining the CD I'd just given him. Miles sat down next to him. "This is dope, Mamie. I'm so ready to get some more stuff recorded. Get this thing movin'!"

"What y'all got goin' on?" Miles inquired curiously, taking the CD out of Tre's hand.

"Mamie makes the beats and I spit the rhymes," Tre said.

"We do what we do," I said modestly.

"Thas whassup!" Miles gave Tre a pound. "A female producer, like Missy Elliott?"

"Yeah, but better! I'm that *new* flava in ya ear," I said.

"DJ Ill Mama's off the hiz-zook, playa," Tre said. I loved getting my props, and Tre definitely gave me my props.

"Do you spit crazily too?" I asked.

"Nah, sounds like I'd better leave that to cuz." Miles gave Tre another pound.

"Check this out." Tre handed Miles his iPod. "Just press play. It's some of the freshness we got poppin' off in the DMV."

"DMV?" Miles asked.

"DC, Maryland, Virginia, cuz. You gotta get with the East Coast lingo now!" They high-fived and Miles popped Tre's earbuds in and immediately began nodding his head to the beat. Tre and I continued.

"Seriously, what we doin', Mamie? What's up wit your boys? I can't believe Blue still hasn't called me back. I ain't chasin' nobody down."

"I feel you. Blue's sayin' Blue Up is a wrap. He and Collin are having some problems. The drama at the party the other night was a little setback. I need to get with Collin, though, for the real scoop."

"Yeah, I was shocked when you sent me that text, and then the news about Whiteboy. I hope he gets better soon, but in the meantime we gotta still be about business. All I know is, just since the party, heads are hittin' me up on Facebook, and I'm gettin' mad calls from managers and invites to book shows. I'm all for loyalty, but if Blue Up is really a wrap, we gotta get this, Mamie." Tre let out a long exhale.

"I know, Tre. I'm looking at it like a small glitch. But I've been thinking we should go ahead and do a mix CD. While Blue and Collin figure it out. I'm actually trying to make something happen at Right Trak Studios. I may be able to get us some time for a steal," I said, patting his arm.

"How'd you hook that up?"

"Hook what up?" Miles said, removing the earbuds. "Your flow is ridiculous, cuz, and I'm feelin' you, DJ Ill Mama."

"We might be goin' in the studio," Tre said.

"Y'all need to with the quickness. This sound is on that next level." Miles nodded.

"I've got a little cash, and Whiteboy's dude Loc looked out. I've been texting since the party. Turns out your boy Rook, who Whiteboy does the artwork for, paid for a crapload of studio time but skipped out."

"Yeah, I know he straight disappeared. Cool, let's book it. That fool never paid me the last of my money for that hook

I laced him with. As far as I'm concerned, he owes me."

"So far Loc is sayin' all I have to do is come up with five hundred dollars. I've got three fifty of it," I said.

"Cuz, I might be able to help you. I've got about a hundred fifty."

"Miles, I appreciate it, but I don't have that kinda cash to pay you back."

"Yeah, me either," I added.

"Consider it an investment. I'll make my money back when we sell the mix CD. You are gonna sell it, right?" Miles asked.

"I hadn't thought about that," I said.

"I gotta do this. The music is too hot. I may not know everybody you're talkin' about, but it doesn't sound like you need them. Sounds more like y'all need *me* to be your business manager."

"I'm down if cuz got the cash," Tre agreed.

"Trevaughn and Miles, c'mon in here!" Tre's grandmother shouted from inside the house.

"Aunt Sweets don't play, does she?" Miles laughed. "I'll meet you inside, cuz. Mamie, I look forward to kickin' it," he said, licking his lips, eyeing me up and down. "Think about what I said." He winked. Damn, Tre's cousin was kinda fly.

"Yo, Romeo, can you turn that down?" Tre snapped.

I added, "Yeah, Cold-Rock-Tha-Party Cali. We'll be talkin'." We all shared a laugh at the nickname I came up with for Miles.

"Aw, y'all got jokes!" Miles jumped up and made just as grand an exit as his entrance was.

"Sorry, Miles has always been like that." We exchanged light laughter as he stood up. Tre shot me a sweet look. I didn't know who was more adorable, him or Miles.

"I'll holla when I get the studio set up." I gave Tre a hug.

"Don't leave me hangin', Mamie. I want this cake too bad."

"Trevaughn!" His grandmother yelled louder this time.

"I feel you," I said, checking my cell. "I'm out."

"Yeah, I've got crazy homework. I'll check the new stuff out and hit you." Tre tossed his backpack over his shoulder. "Yo, Mamie, you got the hot tracks and I got notebooks filled with dope lyrics. It's all about striking while the irons are hot!" he shouted on his way inside.

Aunt Deb had a billboard of a news flash for me waiting when I walked in the front door . . .

"Aunt Deb, what's all my stuff doing at the door!" I shouted, walking into the house. All my belongings had been boxed up and neatly stacked at the door.

"Mamie, life is not a game. I keep telling you. The school notified me that you're on probation; you barely show up. So you need to work out your issues. I paid my own way through college and nursing school. I don't have sympathy for slackers. You've got something special, but you don't realize it. And it ain't this music crap! You've got brains. But I'm too tired. I'm tired of talking until I'm blue in the face.

"So here's your chance to be grown and figure it out. You

can't be here and not do your job, and that's going to school," she said, putting down the last box. It was filled with all my CDs. "I need my key," she said, stone-faced.

"Where am I supposed to go?" I said through gritted teeth, my eyes pooling up with a vicious round of tears.

"Anywhere but here until you can get yourself and your priorities together." I handed her the key and began to load up my car with the boxes.

When she closed the door, I knew she was serious. What was I going to do now? I had no particular destination. I guessed I could go to the club to kill some time, but then what? I found myself pulling into the parking lot of Jade's apartment building and shot her a quick text:

HEY GIRLIE WHERE U @?

A few seconds later she replied:

@ HOSP W/MOMS 2NITE WHASSUP?

I fired back:

COOL GIVE HER A HUG FOR ME!

I didn't even bother telling her what was going on with me. My girl had enough to worry about with her mom. I contemplated calling Collin, but after that last salty text he sent me, I decided against it. I figured the parking lot was a safe spot for tonight. She wasn't home, but I knew the neighborhood.

I locked my doors and reclined my seat. I was beat. I pulled out my wallet and counted out four hundred dollars. Three fifty had to go for studio time. That was all I had to my name. Wow, things were pretty jacked-up, but I had one thing working . . . I had a dream. And I was willing to spend everything I had on it. Aunt Deb would see. I said a silent prayer . . .

God, I know I don't do this very often, but I'm scared this time. If you could just look out for me, that would be real cool.

I closed my eyes tightly and cried myself to sleep.

CHAPTER NINE

BLUE

Now ... what y'all wanna do?
Wanna be ballers? Shot-callers?
—Puff Daddy, "It's All About the Benjamins"

I know it sounds bad, but I hadn't been back to the hospital to see Whiteboy since the night Collin and I got into it. That was a week ago. It's not like I wasn't praying for him or anything, but I'm sorry, I needed to put some distance between myself and the situation. Besides, what could visiting him really do? He wouldn't even know I was there. I felt bad that I never checked the messages and missed that call from the hospital, but between getting my pops and Rico off my back, I just couldn't get consumed in Whiteboy's situation.

Although I'd managed to start getting things in order at school, I still didn't have a clue about what the hell I was going to say to Rico in less than twelve hours. I was stressing

so much about the meeting, my stomach was in knots.

"Morning, Mom," I said, dragging myself to the breakfast table.

"Blue, honey, you okay?" Mom said with a frown as she stuffed a stack of graded papers into her tote bag.

"Just an upset stomach or something." I gave her an uneasy look.

"I haven't heard you talk too much lately about your friend Whiteboy. Is that what's bothering you? I'm still shocked about him being in a coma. Did they ever find the boys who did that to him?"

"Nah, not yet," I quickly replied. I never told my parents the whole truth about what happened to Whiteboy. I just said he had been jumped by some random guys. You know, sort of a wrong place at the wrong time type situation. Pops was already buggin' out. If they'd known it was the result of a fight at *my* party I might *never* have been able to leave the house.

"Lord, that's why I worry about you hanging with that boy. He's had such a rough life," she said, shaking her head.

"But, Mom, that's his past, and you always say a person can change if given a chance."

"I know, baby, and I meant that," she said, letting out a sigh. "I'm sorry for being unfair. This is a tough time for you. Whiteboy is a good kid and very talented. Listen, I know you haven't been to see him lately, and I think you should. I realize he doesn't have much of a family. They say even when people are in that state, they can feel the presence of loved ones, and some-times even hear things. Why don't you go today after school?"

"I can't. Remember, I've gotta volunteer at the rec center. Today's my first day," I said, pouring myself a glass of juice. "Did you remind Dad?" I nervously tapped my foot. I was keeping my fingers crossed that he wouldn't throw a wrench in things. I couldn't miss that meeting with Rico.

"I'll remind him. I'm sure it'll be okay. But as far as White-boy, you make sure you get there tomorrow. Stop putting it off."

"Yes, ma'am," I said, taking a sip from my glass. "So, um, where is Dad this morning?" I asked hesitantly.

"He'll be down in a bit. You sure you feel okay?" she asked, putting the palm of her hand on my forehead. "On second thought, maybe you've got that bug that's been going around."

"Nah, Mom, I don't think so," I nervously chuckled.

"Well, by the way, I was pretty angry at you after that party nonsense, but I know you've heard enough from your dad. I think in time this will all pass. Taking the money out of your account was unacceptable, but there's no sense in both of us harping on this mess. Now it's about you honoring your word. Showing him how seriously you take your future." She patted me on the top of my head.

Just then my father landed in the kitchen. I felt a chill when he zoomed past me.

"Blue's not feeling well, David," she added, grabbing her bag and coffee thermos.

"Yeah, well, he'd better get it together!" my father sharply replied, sitting down at the other end of the table and gulping down his coffee. He shot a hard glare in my direction. I swallowed a lump in my throat. "Because you *won't* be missing school today!"

"David, is that really necessary? Nobody said anything about him missing school," my mother snapped.

"Yeah, whatever . . ." The rest of his grumblings were inaudible as he stood up and snatched his newspaper off the table. "Make sure you get to school *on time*. And it's been a week; I wanna see some results, called *good grades*, soon!" he warned one last time, grabbing his briefcase and storming out of the kitchen.

Moments later the slam of the front door jolted both my mom and me, further punctuating what was sure to be the worst day of my life. I let out a deep breath and buried my face in my hands.

"Blue, things will get better."

"But yo, Mom, Dad won't even talk to me, and when he does, he's yelling. What should I do?"

"Blue, you've broken our trust, but like I told you, it'll pass." She gave me a reassuring look. "Come right home after the rec center," she said, scooting away from the table. "C'mon, I'll give you a break from the Metro and drop you at school."

I grabbed my backpack and followed her out of the house.

* * *

The opulence of Rico's office seemed to swallow me up. I felt myself sweating. My Sidekick buzzed. I quickly checked it. Damn, it was just a Facebook message with a friend request:

MISCHA aka CLUB GIRL ADDED YOU AS A FRIEND ON FACEBOOK. WE NEED TO CONFIRM THAT YOU KNOW MISCHA aka CLUB GIRL . . .

Blah, blah, blah . . .

She couldn't be serious. Not only did she ruin things with my girl Jade, this chick was relentless. I rejected the request and shut off my phone. For real, I thought it might have been Collin apologizing for runnng scared, making a last-minute effort to show some support at least. He owed me! Dude had totally left me hanging.

"My man Blue Reynolds!" Rico's grand entrance from behind shook me a bit.

"Hey, Rico," I said, standing up. My knees felt wobbly. "How was your trip to Cali?" I nervously asked.

"Have a seat." He nodded. "Cali was cool. It always is. Looks like I'm going to be opening a spot out there. But let's get on with the business at hand." So much for small talk. "Where's your partner in crime?"

"Well, um, we kind of put things on hiatus for a minute," I cracked.

"Ah, hiatus, I see." He laughed. "Sometimes business and friends don't mix, huh?"

"I guess so."

"So then it looks like you've got some settling up to do with me, personally. You owe me for damages."

"Right, but I was wondering about the money we made?"

"What money? Yo, Blue, the only reason I even allowed you to come to my office is because you got heart. But you were in over your head. You had no control of your own event. That's the number one rule in this game. Five hundred people at twenty bucks a pop, you could've been sitting on some lovely change."

"Tell me about it."

"Ten Gs could've set you up in real business with me. The bottom line, these things don't just go away, and that wasn't enough to cover the damage or my time. So I did you a favor by taking your profits. And since I'm feeling nice today, I'm going to give you a discount. You only owe me another five Gs in outstanding damages."

My eyes went wide. Where was this dude getting his figures from? "Rico, with all due respect, I realize a few chairs were thrown, maybe some broken glasses, but not fifteen Gs' worth! How do you expect me to come up with the extra money?" I snapped. "I've gotta be honest. I'm broke and I can't go to my parents on this one. I actually owe them five hundred bucks."

"You wanted to be in the big-time."

"But, Rico, I don't have the money to pay you back. C'mon!" I pleaded.

"Look, time is money. How are we gonna settle this?" he said matter-of-factly.

He wanted an answer right now, but my brain was frozen. Five Gs was a joke. I didn't have that kind of money. All of a sudden, Chuck's words came back to me like some kind of divine message: *Be honest, be humble, your best asset is you.*

"Blue, I don't have all night. What are we doing about settling this score?"

At that point I decided to throw caution to the wind. To go for it. Sounding stupid couldn't be any worse than looking as stupid as I did right now. "Well, Rico, um, look, I know I have a lot to learn and I screwed up big-time. You're right I was in over my head, but I know I can be successful at this game. You gave me a shot and opened a door for me.

"I need a cat like you to show me how to win. I don't have any money, but I have my brain, I've got an eye for talent, and I'm willing to learn." I paused and swallowed hard. "I'd like to work the money off. I'll do anything—pass out promotional items, flyers, run errands for you, *anything*. Maybe even like a protégé in the making," I said, cracking a smile. I was desperate.

"First off, slow down. Never tell *anybody* that you'll do *anything*." Rico leaned in closer to me. "I gotta give you credit. You've got balls, and that's better than guts sometimes." He laughed. "So what are you going to do about school?"

"I'll work it in."

"Okay, see, check it: If you're gonna be my protégé, it's not about *working* school in. I've *survived* in this game because I got one degree from the Hood University, but I've *thrived* because of college and an MBA."

"I heard, Harvard." I felt about as small as an ant.

"You seem like you have some decent parents. What do they say about all this?"

"They aren't too happy with me right now. My dad was actually cool with me doing the party thing at first, but he's upset right now about how I'm not focused enough on school and college."

"So you're one of those privileged young brothas, huh?"

"Nah, it's not like that. My dad's a lawyer, but he paid his way through law school. He followed in my grandfather's footsteps. He actually wants me to attend his alma mater, Howard. I may not do the college thing, though."

"May not *do* the college thing? You may have just blown this meeting. Let me tell you something, Blue. It's stupid thinking like that. It produces quitters and failures, two types of people I don't like very much. When I was your age I didn't have the opportunities you have. My parents didn't have money to send me to school. My father worked himself into an early grave. I grew up in the hood, right here in DC, where my choices were to either live a life that would most likely end before I saw my twenty-first birthday or bust my ass and make something of myself."

"Wow, I feel you," I said with a sobering expression.

"I had sense enough to know that I couldn't make something of myself without an education. And all I knew was that I never wanted to see my mother work another night shift for crumbs. I see a lot of myself in you. So check this out: I'm going to give you one last chance. Weekends, Friday and Saturday nights, to work off your debt, and just like your pops is puttin' that pressure on you, I expect you to put a hundred percent toward handling your school business too. If you're gonna be down with Rico Tate, then you've gotta be smart."

"Okay, I'm cool with it!" He didn't have to tell me twice.

"So whassup with the deejay girl and the rapper kid?"

"What do you mean?"

"I mean, that kid is amazing and so is the deejay. Take a tip from me. They got people talkin'. Having talent makes you valuable. Make sure you've got your business with them taken care of."

"Fo sho! I've got contracts!" We gave each other a pound to seal the deal. "By the way, when do I start?"

"I was wondering when you'd ask that." He smirked, putting on his shades. "One of my people from the club will call you. Just be ready!"

When I stepped outside the doors of Club Heat, where Rico's office was housed, I was hyped. I looked up at the club's marquee and broke into a victory dance. I was about to be ballin' uncontrollably!

I was hyped the whole Metro ride home, blastin' my iPod

the entire way. I killed the power and removed my earphones when I saw my pops's car in the driveway—it was a sobering reminder that I had to chill. I was suddenly panic-stricken, praying that my mother hadn't forgotten to tell him I had been to the rec center. I definitely didn't need any drama with him tonight.

I cautiously entered the house. "Dad?" I called out. I could hear the television playing in his study.

"In the office," he yelled back.

"Hey," I said hesitantly, poking my head in. He was busy organizing paperwork.

"I'm headed to New York in the morning and I don't want any monkey business while I'm away," he sternly replied. "And by the way, you'd better not pull anymore slick moves like the one you just pulled." My heart was pounding and beads of nervous sweat began to form on my forehead. I just knew he'd found out that I'd lied about going to the rec center, and he was about to bust me out about meeting with Rico Tate.

"Don't ever try to play your mom and me against each other. I think the rec center is admirable, but making the grades is more important right now. Also, you talked to your mom about going to see your friend at the hospital. I may be angry with you, but I'm sympathetic about Whiteboy's condition. Just remember you have responsibilities at home. I've had some second thoughts. I'm going to agree to you making hospital visits in addition to the library and academic-related activities, but that's it! We'll see how this school stuff starts to shake out before you can volunteer at the center."

"Yes, sir." I was relieved.

"You're excused. Get on those books!"

"Yes, sir." I swiftly made my way to my room, where I plopped down on my bed and cracked open my biology book. A smile crept across my face. *Hells yes!* I was so on. I knew I was going to have to work my butt off to juggle school, my new internship, *and* my parents, but I was back. I'd just proved I didn't need Collin or anybody else. I'd show Collin that Blue Up could've been a reality with him. Too bad he bailed. I was officially Rico Tate's protégé! Just give me time. My star was definitely going to shine.

CHAPTER TEN

Bam, boom, watchoo gone do cuz?
Guess I'm rollin' in with them baby blue Chucks
—Snoop Dogg, "From tha Chuuuch to Da Palace"

I'd been waiting for my cousin Miles in the Duke Ellington student lounge for almost an hour. I was heated. He'd been in town barely twenty-four hours and he was already up to something. I could feel it. Miles was mad cool, but he was the kind of dude that was always scheming. I remembered my moms used to take me to visit him every summer in Cali, and even back in the day when we were shorties he could hustle me out of everything from my Hot Wheels to bubble gum.

Sweets *made* me bring him with me to school today. I didn't have a chance to argue or question it. Yesterday, Miles just popped up. Sweets gave me the same line he did about him just "visiting" for a while. Then she sprang it on me this morning

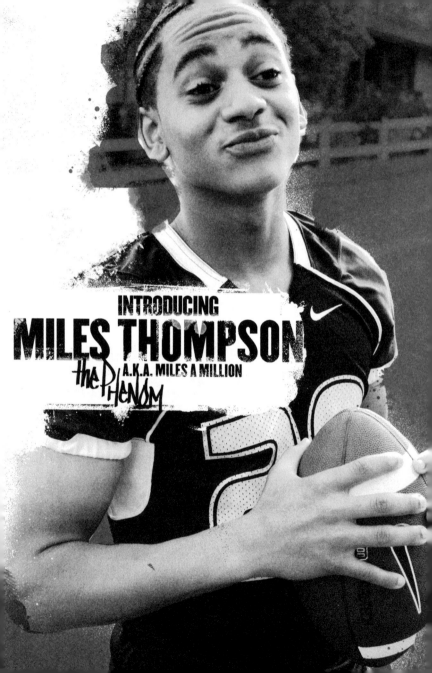

INTRODUCING

MILES THOMPSON

the Phenom   A.K.A. MILES A MILLION

that she had arranged for him to go to school with me during his stay. On the real, as chill as I thought it might be having my cousin around, I was skeptical of the whole thing. Sweets was definitely hiding something.

It was too awkward to talk about anything last night, plus I'd had to finish studying for a big music theory test. I checked my watch again. When Miles told me he'd meet me in fifteen minutes after last period, I warned him not to be late. If I missed the next bus, I was gonna flip. My cell buzzed, alerting me I had a text message:

WHASSUP? HOLLA @ UR BOY
—BLUE

Oh, that fool must be joking. Whatever! I guessed he *finally* decided I was worthy enough to call back. I must've called him a million times since that party. I'd gotten nothing in return and now he wouldn't. I deleted his message and checked the time *again*. Okay, it was a wrap. I was out. Sweets was just going to have to be mad, oh well. Miles would have to figure out how to get home on his own. I had things to do tonight, mainly puttin' in some time on my music. I was diggin' Mamie's new tracks and I'd already come up with some blazin' new lyrics. I was feigning to get in the studio.

My cell buzzed again.

YO NOT TRYIN' 2 SWEAT U BUT HIT ME BACK
—HOLLA BLUE

Was he serious? He just texted me like two minutes ago. I ignored the message, put my headphones on, and exited the lounge, making my way down the main hallway of the school.

As I headed toward the front entrance, I passed the auditorium and stopped to check out the poster for the upcoming musical. I had to do a major double take when I spotted two people making out in the far corner. Oh, wow! It was Miles. He was in the middle of a serious tongue-down with a honey, oblivious to the outside world. I rolled up on them stealth-like. Dang, cuz hadn't wasted any time getting to know the honeys around here.

A soon as I was just a few feet away, I held my hands up to my mouth like a bullhorn and shouted, "Ay, yo, Miles!" I scared the crap out of them. He was cold busted, and babygirl turned three shades of red in the face. She looked vaguely familiar. He wasted no time scooping her up.

"Oh, my bad, cuz," Miles said, wiping his mouth. "Leslie, this is my cousin Tre." He snickered.

"Um, it's Lisa," she said, cutting her eyes at him. "Hey. You know, I think we have drama together," she said, flush with embarrassment, wiping her mouth.

"Yeah, yeah, we do. Well, um, nice to meet you." The awkwardness of the moment left us all speechless.

"O-kay, um, I'd better go," Lisa said, rushing off.

"I'mma hit you later, boo!" Miles called out, giving me dap. "Yo, I love this school!" he proudly proclaimed, holding his arms out like he was on top of the world.

"Playa, you know you were about to get straight left!" I said, shaking my head. "I guess I can't be *that* mad at you after all. Man, first day at a new school, I'd say it was a good day." We laughed, giving each other dap.

"A real good day, and in the immortal words of Snoop D.O. double G, 'pimpin' ain't easy,' but it sho is necessary!" I shook my head, but I had to give him some dap on his game.

Between waiting for Miles and the nearly two-hour commute home, I was definitely ready to escape into my music. We hopped off the bus and started walking home. A block later and Miles was still complaining about the long ride from Duke Ellington to Anacostia.

"Yo, cuz, this is crazy. Why do you take all those buses just to go to school?" He frowned.

"Fool, it's not just *any* school. It's the best school for the arts in DC, maybe the country for that matter," I explained.

"Well, it seems fruity as hell up in that joint! And you'd better tell Auntie, I ain't about to put on no tights and ballet shoes!" We laughed and gave each other high fives. A few feet from the house, Miles stopped me.

"So, yo, cuz, I meant to ask you, whassup with babygirl?"

"You mean Lisa from school?"

"Nah, pimpin', the deejay babe. Mary's her name, right?"

"Dude, it's *Mamie!*" I corrected, shaking my head. "You are so not on your game when it comes to names!"

"My bad, Mamie. Whatever! Just whassup wit her? She's fine. I might wanna get at that," he said confidently.

"Ain't happenin'," I said, waving him off. "She's focused on her music. Plus, you didn't even remember her name. Yo, she ain't about that weak-ass game you be runnin'."

"Hold up, you blockin'?" he said, giving me a playful jab.

"C'mon." I smirked. "Bustas block, I'm lookin' out for a friend, and that's what she is," I said, playing off the conversation, walking off.

"You need to look out for *family* is what you *need* to do! So, what, you got that 'friends with benefits' thing goin' on?" he called out, catching up with me.

We entered the house, and Miles headed straight for the television. I made a beeline for the stairs on a mission to knock out my homework and get into Mamie's CD.

"Trevaughn and Miles, come in the kitchen!" Sweets yelled, stopping me in my tracks.

"Yes, ma'am," we both called back. I wasn't in the mood. I had things to do and Miles had already put me behind schedule.

"Sit down," she said when we made it to the kitchen. She pointed to the table and we all sat down. "What took you boys so long coming home today?" she asked, eyeing both of us suspiciously.

"I had a meeting after school," I quickly spoke up, covering for Miles.

"You know better, Trevaughn. Next time call and tell me something. I was gettin' worried. Now listen," she said. "I didn't get to talk to you boys last night, but, Trevaughn, Miles is going to be staying with us for a while. And, Miles, we do things a little different than in California. Your mama said you've been hangin' out late with a rough crowd and not doing well in school." Miles rolled his eyes.

"None of that," she reprimanded. "Now, your mama is my only sister's child. I'm your great-aunt, Miles, but more like your grandmother now that your grandmother has passed away. I told your mama to stop worrying and just send you on here to be with Trevaughn. So I'm warning you, me and your uncle ain't gonna tolerate no monkey business around here. We got rules. You understand?"

"Yeah," he mumbled. I was a little shocked by how nonchalant he was. Cuz just didn't know what he was in for.

"Oh, no. I don't think I heard you 'cause there's a way to address your elders in this house," Sweets snapped.

"Errum, yes, ma'am," he said, clearing his throat and straightening up in his seat.

"So, y'all are excused. Go on up to your room, and both of you get started on some homework. I know you didn't have time last night, Trevaughn, but get that other closet cleaned out in your room for Miles. The airline delivered the rest of his luggage while y'all were at school. Dinner will be ready in a bit."

"Yes, ma'am," I said. Sweets gave Miles a hard stare.

We exited the kitchen and picked up his suitcases, which were stacked by the staircase.

"Yo, thanks for havin' my back in there," he said, giving me a pound.

"I don't like lying to Sweets, Miles. So don't make it a habit."

"Aunt Sweets be breakin' fools off like that. What is this, like jail or something?" He chuckled, following me up the stairs.

"Sweets be keepin' it real. She don't play that," I said, placing his bag down on what had suddenly become his side of the room.

"So now that we can finally talk, what's poppin' on the East Coast? What are we gonna get into tonight?" Miles plopped down on the twin bed adjacent to mine.

"You trippin', right? It's called studying for school, then working on this," I said, holding up my iPod and Mamie's CD. "I'm tryin' to really blow up one day." I sat down at my desk.

"Word! I feel you. I think about blowin' up one day too."

"For real? Doin' what, hustlin'?" I joked.

"Nah, seriously, football," he said, walking over to his duffel bag and pulling out a football. "I'm nice like that. I might even go pro one day," He tossed it in the air.

"Well, from what Sweets said, you'd better get them grades up or you're gonna be playin' pro for some parking lot or something!" I got a kick out of my own joke.

"Whatever man! I got a plan."

"What kind of plan?"

"To get that paper in the meantime, fool. I just need to hook up with the right folks now that I'm in DC."

"Miles, c'mon, quit buggin'. That ain't my flow. My hustle is school and my music."

"Then do you. I ain't mad at a playa. Personally, I think all this school stuff is corny. All I need is the speed in these feet." He nodded down at his feet. "And in these hands." He tossed his football again and caught it. "So whassup? I need to get it crackin'."

"Whatever, man. I need to get it crackin' on this homework. I've gotta finish studying for this calculus test. This class is kicking my butt big-time," I said, opening my book.

"Calculus ain't hard." He laughed.

"Yeah, okay, Miles!" I retorted.

"But yo, I'm serious, you gonna hook me up with the playas around here so I can get my hustle on?"

"Sweets is gonna love that! You'll be shipped back to Cali so fast your head will be spinnin'. Look, you might wanna slow ya roll around here. I told you I'm strictly about gettin' my work done and puttin' in work on my gift," I bragged, pretending to brush imaginary dirt off my shoulders.

"Thas whassup. Sounds like you need a manager." He nodded, flashing a grin.

"I'm supposed to have one, but some stuff is goin' down right now. I gotta get it figured out."

"Well, when you do, let me know. I might be able to help you out. I'm pretty good at makin' moves. In the meantime, I gotta talk to Aunt Sweets about gettin' me into a *real* school. No offense, but Duke Ellington is not really my flow," he cracked.

"Maybe you need to be more open-minded. You saw, we've got classes like regular high school. It's just in the afternoons we focus on the arts, like music, art, theater, dance. Don't sleep."

"Yeah, well, ain't no football team, problem numero uno. But there *are* some bangin' babes up in there!"

"We should check and see if you can get in one of the leagues around here," I suggested.

"That'll be cool. I was the star running back in the league I play in back home," he said wistfully.

"You think you're gonna miss LA?"

"Hecks yeah, but I don't have a choice *but* to be here. It's all temporary, though. In the meantime, I gotta get my hustle and grizzle on fo shizzle, right?" We gave each other dap.

"Trevaughn and Miles, come and eat!"

"Let's kick it while I'm here, and maybe you'll stop blockin' with Mamie. Yeah, DJ Ill Mama." He was practically salivating.

"Yeah, kick it." I gave him a hearty fist pound. But his comment about me so-called blockin' rubbed me the wrong way. I ain't hatin', but Mamie was too good for him. Damn, why did I suddenly feel protective of her?

CHAPTER ELEVEN

BLUE

Less stuntin', more fame, less talkin', more change
—Talib Kweli, "More or Less"

I think the planets were *finally* lining up in my favor. Moms and Pops had both left before I woke up. Moms slipped a note under my door.

Blue,
I've got parent-teacher conferences after school this
week and Dad left for New York this morning on an
early train for a weeklong conference. Eat leftovers.

love, Mom

PS-Keep this between us but you can use my car for school,
the library, and the hospital only. You're still grounded!

Life was real sweet right about now. Mom's note was the perfect wake-up call to kick-start my day. I breezed through my morning classes and was coasting through the afternoon. I was feeling so good I even chose to spend my free period in the library. That was a big step for a brotha like me. Just twenty-four hours after Rico put me down, I was inspired to turn a new page. If making good grades got me in his inner circle and kept my dad off my back, then honor roll make room! I was about to be juggling a lot, but I was in it to win it, and like Jay-Z said, I got my swagger back!

I was just anxious for things to get started. I was also anxious about Jade. I couldn't help it. I missed her bad. She was the one person I wished I could share everything that was going on with me to. I wondered if she really meant what she said about wanting me to leave her alone. You know sometimes when people say no, they really mean yes. Us being apart had to have been killing her too, right? I decided to text her.

JUST CHECKIN' ON MOMS . . . U COOL?

I took a deep breath and pressed send. I sat for several minutes, impatiently staring at the screen. *Man, if she'd just hit me back and say something*, I thought. I was just about to give up when a message from Jade flashed:

THANX SHE'S HANGIN' IN THERE . . . TTYL!

She was brief, but hey, at least she responded. Maybe I could change her mind about us. I was gonna stay hopeful that working with Rico would put me in a position to one day show her how good it could be between us. She couldn't have meant all that stuff about wanting me to leave her alone. I definitely had a lot to prove. I knew I'd made some mistakes, and I was fighting the doubters big-time. But hey, if Diddy made it, so could I!

The only thing buggin' me out was that Rico said to "be ready," but he didn't give me much else to go on. I felt like I was in limbo waiting for *the* call. And what made it worse, Tre hadn't hit me back. I couldn't believe I'd been checking my phone for messages like every five minutes all day. I admit, as far as Tre was concerned, I probably didn't handle things the best way. I flaked on him and Mamie. I was gonna fix that situation, though. I just needed him to give me another shot.

My phone buzzed:

IT'S CHUCK WHEN U COMIN' TO THE CENTER WE NEED U

I didn't have an answer for Chuck. He was the only glitch in this whole equation. I had given him my word, but volunteering at the rec center was quickly moving down my list of priorities. I was going to get to him, but first it was about gettin' what Whiteboy calls "grimy." I shot him back a quick reply:

POPS WANTS TO SEE SOME GRADES FIRST
BUT THEN I'M ON IT

At least I could stall him with the pops excuse. I needed to have tunnel vision right now—school, bustin' my ass for Rico, and getting Blue Up back and running. The rec center was on hold in my mind. It was time to show and prove, move forward, and cut the haters.

Just then Collin entered the library. Seeing him triggered a sharp tug in my gut. Speaking of haters. I couldn't believe he was headed in my direction. I defensively shifted in my chair.

"Whassup?" he coolly asked.

"'Sup?" I nonchalantly replied.

"Listen, I don't wanna make a big deal, but I've been going to see Whiteboy pretty much every day. I don't know whassup, but I know you haven't been to the hospital in a while and I think you need to go check him out."

"Yeah, well, I've been tied up, and I had to handle some important business *yesterday*. You know with Rico Tate. Don't trip, I'm not about to run away from *my* word!"

"Yo, you gotta deal with your own conscience," he said, letting out a puff of air. "I just wanted to put it out there, since your *word* is so important. And to think I was going to apologize about the confrontation in the hospital parking lot. I'm glad I didn't. By the way, it's about Whiteboy, not either of us."

"You done?" I tossed him the peace sign and swiveled in my

seat, returning to my studies. Collin had no choice but to walk away after my silent dis. I noticed he settled at a table across the room. He had major balls steppin' to me like that. I didn't need his punk ass reminding me about *my* homeboy being laid up in the hospital. I hadn't forgotten. How could I forget that Whiteboy was in a coma? But I had to do *me* for a minute. Until I could get things rollin' again.

I tried to refocus on the chapter I had been reading before I was *rudely* interrupted, but Collin had put me in a foul mood. I could see him in my peripheral view. I put my headphones on to tune him out, but I wasn't feelin' the whole library vibe anymore. I tossed down my pencil, leaned my head back, closed my eyes, and rolled my shoulders to decompress.

I started thinking about Blue Up and what I needed to do to show Collin how *real* playas do it. Getting in with Rico may have been the first step, but without Mamie and Tre in pocket I was back at ground zero. I figured since Tre wasn't hitting me back, maybe Mamie would. I whipped out my phone and shot a text off to her.

WHERE U @? HIT YA BOY BLUE

A few minutes passed and still no response. I inconspicuously peeped at Collin again. He was hard at work. I couldn't let him win this war. I decided to head home. Just then my phone vibrated.

B @ THE CLUB 2MORROW NITE @ 11 REPORT TO BIG MIKE—RT

Sweet! I quickly stuffed my books into my backpack. My phone vibrated again. It was from Mamie:

OH NOW U WANNA TALK????

I quickly fired back.

YO I'M SORRY, BUT I GOT GOOD NEWS I'M BACK BABY!

AND????? WHATEVR

She typed a series of sad faces and squiggly lines.

LOOK SORRY ABOUT THE PAST BUT BLUE UP IS BACK . . . I'M ROLLIN' SOLO & GONNA BE WORKING FOR RICO. U DOWN

MAYBE . . . NO FRONTIN' THIS TIME

IT'S ALL GOOD SO WHASSUP!!!!

U'D BETTA BE 4REAL YO U NEED TO GET WITH TRE IF HE'S IN THEN I'M IN

I GOT U . . . I'M GONNA TRY TO SCOOP HIM NOW HOLLA IN A MINUTE

K . . . HANDLE YOUR B.I. TTYL! . . .
DJ ILL MAMA GOT THE FI-YAH TO TAKE U HI-YAH

I hurriedly scooped up my backpack, flung it over my shoulder, and raced out, leaving Collin in my dust.

Moms letting me use the car while Pops was away worked out perfectly. Moms always had a soft spot for me. It didn't hurt that she worried about me riding the Metro. I milked it for everything I could. I mean, the Metro isn't bad, but if it's a choice between the train and my own wheels, I'll take the car any day.

I hopped in my car and jetted, headed in the direction of Tre's school. I was even going to track him down at his house if I had to. Despite traffic, I made it across town in record time and spotted Tre sitting at a crowded bus stop, wearing his headphones and bobbing his head.

"Yo, Tre!" I said, slowing to a stop next to the bus stop where he was sitting, honking and waving out of the sunroof. He stood up with a major attitude and folded his arms across his chest. "I've been texting you, playa. Why haven't you hit me back?" I yelled across the seat, out the passenger's window.

"For real? Nah, bro, I don't recall a text from you, bro," Tre said, waving me off.

"Who's this fool, cuz?" shouted a slim but athletic-looking dude sporting a heavy West Coast drawl and cornrows, rushing to stand guard next to him.

"Oh, *this* fool." Tre snickered. "This *was* my dude, the infamous

Blue Reynolds of Blue Up, we can make you blow up, Productions," he mocked. "Yo, B, I thought you were supposed to be lookin' out for me, you know, puttin' me in the music game."

I put the car in park, flashed my hazards, and got out. "Okay, I deserve that, Tre. I been dealin' with a lot and I'm finally able to see clearly again. I just need to holla at you for a minute. If you don't like what I'm sayin', I'm out." I gave a surrendering gesture, putting my palms up.

"Yo, you got five minutes before my bus gets here." Tre motioned for Miles to follow him over to the car. "Blue, this is my cousin Miles. He just moved here from Cali." They gave me a round of halfhearted pounds.

"Word? LA?" I asked, trying to make small talk, but his cousin wasn't feelin' me.

"Long Beach, pimpin'. Tre, you'd better tell ya boy he shouldn't roll up on folks like that. That's how you get smoked where I'm from!"

"Word!" Tre chimed in, checking his watch. "Okay, now you got four minutes." He and Miles gave each other a pound.

"Okay, okay, look, I'm sorry I bailed on you. There was mad drama with the party and Whiteboy. He's in a coma, and I don't know how he'll come out of this."

"Damn, on the real I'm sorry about your boy," Tre said, shaking his head. "But he's gonna get better, no doubt, and let him know I'll be waiting for him to lace me with some new artwork. That cat is strong."

"Yeah, yeah, most def." I gave him a pound.

"I don't know your man, but cuz showed me the artwork he did for him the last time. He's dope," Miles added. "Yo, T, let me hold your iPod while you chop it up." Tre handed it to Miles and he retreated to the bench at the bus stop.

"Like I was sayin, Tre, the good news is that I think stuff is about to turn around." I sat on the hood of the car. "I owe you and Mamie a big apology. You guys were right. I didn't handle my business like I should have. I had to sort of shut the operation down temporarily. Collin did some ill shit, so I don't deal with him anymore."

"Sorry to hear that."

"Don't be. Blue Up was mine from the beginning and always will be. I'm cool with that."

"But that still doesn't change the fact that we had a deal to be straight-up with each other. That *ain't* cool."

"I know and I can explain everything."

"Go ahead," he said with a hint of skepticism.

"Let's just say you're looking at Rico Tate's official protégé. I worked it out to intern for him to settle the debt I owe from the party damages. And as part of the deal he wants to help blow you and Mamie up." I was hyped.

"For real? I mean, like for real, for real?" he said, leaning his head back, still somewhat suspect.

"Word is bond!" I insisted.

"Yo, I need details, dude," Tre unenthusiastically replied.

"Well, I'm not exactly sure yet." Tre rolled his eyes. "No, wait, look, Rico was talking to me about setting up a way for you all to perform, and I might have a show for you at my boy Chuck Davis's new rec center in a couple of months. I'll be working on both."

"Okay, this is hot, but I'm getting all kinds of hits on Facebook about performing *now*. I can't pass that up. Mamie and I are about to work on this mix CD too. She's gonna book some time at Right Trak Studios."

"I realize you can't just sit around. Just bear with me. I can do this thing with Rico and it can be huge. In the meantime, I'm all for you guys recording and putting out a CD, even if you do a show or two, but remember we've gotta deal." I gave him a pound. "I'm grounded right now, but if you guys go in the studio, I'll figure out a way to be there—don't worry. I wish I could pay for the studio time, but I'm broke. All the money I made from the party has to cover the damages."

"Hey, I understand. Mamie said she had the whole studio thing under control. Yo, I gave you my word and I won't get down with any other managers, but whether it's Rico or Chuck or whoever, you've gotta make somebody deliver for real this time," he said, looking me squarely in the eye.

"No doubt!" I jumped off the car and gave him a pound to seal the deal.

"Mamie gave me some new tracks and they're even better than the track that got Rico interested in the first place. We need some heavy hitters to see us and give us a deal."

"Bet! So hop in. I'll drop you guys off!"

"Ay, yo, cuz!" Tre called out to Miles, who was doing a serious head bob to the beat of the bass thumping through is headphones.

"Whassup, T?" he asked, removing them.

"My boy Blue is giving us a ride."

"Cool, 'cause riding the bus is wack! You know I've got an image." We all laughed as they got in the car. "So you straight on the business, T?" Miles asked, climbing into the backseat.

"Real straight!" He nodded. "Let's do this for real this time, Blue!" he said, slamming the door. I hit the stereo and sped off.

CHAPTER TWELVE

COLLIN

**I want the money, money and the cars, cars and the clothes . . .
I just wanna be successful
—Drake featuring Trey Songz, "Successful"**

After school I reported to my father's office as scheduled. As I headed toward one of the cubicles near my father's office, I was intercepted by a young attorney.

"Hey, young Andrews," he said, extending his hand. "I'm Jason Steinbeck. I wanted to introduce myself." I noticed his monogrammed sterling cuff links and slicked-back hair, complete with the designer suit and Italian shoes—definitely not my style. I'd much rather sport a pair of cargos to the courtroom versus Calvin Klein.

"I told your dad I'd show you the ropes," he said with a confident swagger.

"Cool," I said, placing my backpack on the desk.

"Your dad's definitely one of the best, and he plays a helluva golf game. Yeah, I came out of Georgetown Law, and he's like a legend." I nodded, not impressed by his ass-kissing acrobatics. "Listen, I'm shadowing one of the partners on a big case involving the coal industry. Some loser got lung cancer and is trying to blame it on Virginia Coal." He casually sat on the edge of the desk and continued to brag about how the firm was gonna "kill" the guy in court, and then he laughed.

"J, it was good meeting you, but I've gotta hit the books," I said, brushing him off. It was disgusting to hear this asshole laugh at the expense of another human being.

"I'm here for you, bro!" He handed me his card. I tossed it in the can as soon as he turned away. I refocused and sat down, cracking open my history book. We were studying the civil rights movement. The assignment was to write about the politics of the 1960s versus those of today. The struggle people went through back then and the cases lawyers had to try were much more interesting than the crap my dad and his flunkies were doing. It was like the lawyers back then had a purpose. They looked out for people. I scanned the room. I wondered if I would turn into a Jason Steinbeck one day.

My phone buzzed. It was my father sending a text.

DINNER TONIGHT @ THE FOUR SEASONS @ 7

Great. I had to really put on my game face for this one. My father had rescheduled the dinner I missed with the president of

Georgetown. I couldn't disappoint him again. I quickly jumped into my homework. I wanted to make sure I stopped by to see Whiteboy before dinner.

My whole encounter with that attorney at the firm was still bothering me for some reason. I knew it was all about winning cases, because that was how you won the big bucks, but it was like you had to be heartless and cold to do what guys like Jason and my father did. That just ain't me.

I was pensive as I entered Whiteboy's dimly lit room. He at least looked pain free. I tightly gripped the side rail of his bed, until the whites of my knuckles bled through. I gritted my teeth. Here I was about to go to some five-star dinner with some of DC's biggest legal power players, and Whiteboy was on the verge of dying. My dad and probably all of his clients wouldn't even have given a crap about a guy like Whiteboy or what he's been through in life. I guess that's why I've never told my dad about his past. What for? He was too narrow-minded. My dad would just judge him because he can't relate to or understand how Whiteboy turned his life around from hangin' in the streets, gang bangin' and jackin' fools, and being locked up in juvie. But Whiteboy finally realized that was the wrong path and got his life on point, focused on his talents as an artist.

My father condemned the criminal justice system for letting what he called "animals" out of jail. That wasn't right. What about people who just made mistakes, got caught up, and didn't have a family to look out for them, or have the financial resources? I felt like a hypocrite as his son.

"Dude, I'm sorry this happened. I hope you come back soon. Damn, if you only knew how messed up things were." I spoke softly, my head lowered. "I cut ties with Blue. His ego's mad out of control. He's being a real asshole. But it's cool. It's time for me to show the world who Collin Andrews is. I'm not some second-rate sidekick.

"You told me one time never to look back, so that's what I'm doing. I'm going to make things work my father's way. I owe that to him, but I'm doing it for me, too. I've got a plan, and I'm gonna look out for you, too. Just promise you'll get better. It's my time to show everybody what I'm about." I felt a surge of fury run through my veins. It's funny, since Whiteboy's accident, Blue had checked out of not only our friendship but his friendship with Whiteboy. I had to have Whiteboy's back since he always had mine.

The stage was set for the prodigal son as I glided through the glistening dining room at the Four Seasons. Life was moving in slow motion. I was savoring this moment. The tall, shapely honey-colored hostess, who vaguely resembled Shakira, greeted me warmly. She led the way to the private dining room where my father and his colleagues were holed up. Her black cocktail dress framed her well-endowed backside.

I felt as though I had already arrived, like I was some hot-shot young lawyer. My father greeted me with open arms.

"Son, you could've dressed better for the occasion," he chided. I shrugged his comment off and sat down at the table, which was littered with champagne, fine china, and glasses. The room was filled with a cloud of imported-cigar smoke. Everyone was celebrating my father's latest case, a twenty-million-dollar settlement with a large pharmaceutical company.

"This is my son, Collin. He's going to carry the Andrews torch!"

"So, Collin, I hear you have your sights set on Georgetown," the president said, shaking my hand.

"Yes, sir, it's my dream." I beamed.

"We're looking forward to having you in the program this summer. And if you're anything like your father, you're gonna be a killer attorney!" He gave me a hearty pat on the back.

The cork of a champagne bottle exploded out, and it was at that very moment that I realized how much I really *wasn't* like my father. What I did have was his drive, I just had to figure out how to use it to get what *I* wanted.

It was one a.m. and I couldn't sleep. I was still thinking about dinner tonight. I had the brains to get everything my father had and more. The summer couldn't come fast enough. I was itching to get on Georgetown's campus and show everybody what the future looked like—Collin Andrews. I was gonna show Blue too. I'd always had more discipline than him. That was what it took to win. Just then my cell buzzed. It was a text from Mamie:

What the heck was going on?

I raced to the window and opened it. She was in the backyard frantically waving her hands. I quietly raced downstairs, dismantled the alarm, and slipped outside.

"What's wrong?"

"I'm sorry, but I had nowhere else to go. My aunt kicked me out a few nights ago. I've been hanging at the club and sleeping in my car. Jade's been sleeping at the hospital, plus she doesn't need me throwing my crap on her. I don't know what to do." Tears welled up in her eyes.

"Come on," I said, grabbing her hand, leading her into the house.

We made it back to my room without alerting my father. I tossed Mamie one of my T-shirts and a pair of boxers. She slipped them on and climbed into my bed.

"C, I'm sorry about all this. I've just got to figure my life out. I was really banking on Blue Up taking off. I realized school isn't for me. At least not right now. I guess my aunt realized it too. I just need some time—"

"Mamie," I said, cutting her off. "You can crash here until you figure it out. We've got the pool house. I'll get the key in the morning and leave it open for you. My father will never know."

"Thanks, C," she said, wiping her eyes and giving me a hug. "You know, I stopped by the hospital to check on Jade's mom tonight. It's looking real bad for her. How crazy is it that all this is happening? I'm like Mercury must be in retrograde. I read my horoscope."

"I don't know about all that astrological stuff, but I agree. It's like when it rains it pours."

"Tell me about it."

"For me, I just feel like I've lost my sense of direction. I went from running away from everything my father wanted me to do to doing what Blue wanted me to do because I thought his plan was the answer, and now I'm right back where my dad wants me."

"So what *does* Collin want?" she asked.

"Success."

"What else?"

"Happiness. That's the equation I can't quite figure out. How do you get success to equal true happiness? I don't feel like I can have that ultimate level of success and happiness with shitty karma. It's crazy, I feel terrible about what happened to Whiteboy. I feel bad about what happened at the club, and all the money owed to Rico Tate. I feel bad about disappointing you and Tre. I feel—"

"Stop!" Mamie said, cutting me off. "Dude, you're gonna *go* crazy feeling guilty about all this crap. Listen, stuff happens. You shake it off and regroup. As far as Whiteboy, you had nothing to do with that. Fights break out all the time at clubs. And as far as me and Tre, you and Blue just need to get it together."

"I've turned that page for sure, Mamie. I'm done."

"Done? Collin, me and that kid are on fire. Don't you see what Blue Up has with us is golden?" she pleaded.

"Do me a favor and don't mention Blue Up again. It's starting to make me sick."

"Yo, I can hustle, but I need you and Blue. Tre needs you guys. Fools are all over him after seeing him at the club, and he's trying to be loyal. We can do big things together. Plus, truthfully, I have to blow up now more than ever. I got nothing else to bank on. Feel me?"

"Mamie, the one thing you don't ever have to worry about is me. I'm in your corner forever. But I'm an Andrews and some things are just in my DNA. I'm gonna play my father's game for now, mainly for the sake of my mother. She suffered a lot in the last few years of the marriage, and he didn't make things better. She's all good now and eventually got the help she needed when they divorced, stopped taking prescription pills. She's really at peace."

"What do you mean she suffered?" She leaned into me.

"Remember you asked me a long time ago if I had any siblings and I never answered? Well, I did. I *had* a brother."

"Had?"

"Yeah, he was five years older than me. My father's pride. He was the perfect son. Me, I was always going to the beat of my own drum. My father hates that. Kyle was a great athlete and student, but my dad pushed him, sometimes too much. He got into drugs and it was the ugly family secret. He got some bad heroin and the rest is, well, the rest. My dad never forgave my mother. It almost pushed her over the edge too. He blamed her for so much and pushed her away."

"OMG! I had no idea, Collin."

"That's not something you just go around advertising. Blue knows, of course, and now you. My brother was sixteen. His whole life all my father did was talk about Georgetown. I guess I inherited his leftovers. So in a way it's like I've gotta make good on what my brother wasn't able to finish. At the same time Kyle is the wall between me and my dad."

"Collin, just remember you're not in this life thing alone." She grabbed my hand. "You're your own man too. You don't have to live in a shadow anymore." Mamie held my hand in hers and put it up to her heart. Our eyes locked. I felt something and I think she felt it too. Why did I want to kiss her?

"Thanks, Mamie. I needed this more than you know," I said, retraining myself. I took a deep breath. I didn't want to cross the line of friendship, but I was suddenly attracted to her.

"Collin," she said, touching my face. "With your mom's strength and your father's brilliance as a lawyer, you can be unstoppable."

She's your friend, Collin, don't blow this I had to keep telling myself. "Look, you'd better get some rest. Thank you for being here," I said, propping up a pillow for her. "I'm going to work all this out. Things are just crazy, but I know it's temporary. I know I can learn so much from my dad, but he's selfish.

I despise that. That's why I had to walk away from Blue. He was selfish too."

"Okay, I won't disagree with that part about Blue, but he's your best friend. I'm sure he's bummed that you guys aren't talking." She put her other hand up to my cheek, holding my face. "Sometimes you have to be the bigger man."

"I hear everything you're saying, but please let that crap about me and Blue go for once and for all. Anyway, like I said, it's late and we both need rest. Oh, and don't worry about a place to stay. You have one now."

Mamie pecked me on the lips, rolled over, and was knocked out within minutes. I was shocked, holding my fingers to my lips. What did that kiss mean? I was wide awake, paralyzed, a million thoughts floating through my head, fighting to get out, and one of them was my sudden attraction to Mamie.

CHAPTER THIRTEEN

When I met you girl my heart went knock knock
Now them butterflies in my stomach won't stop stop
—Justin Bieber, "One Time"

I wasn't on stalker mode or anything, but when I saw Jade in the Spanish lab studying just four tables away, I had to go over to her. Babygirl looked as beautiful as ever. She was in her own world and didn't notice me. I'm not going to lie. It had been hard. Jade had been on my mind daily, but I was accepting that we weren't together anymore. Maybe when the time was right I'd have another chance. What I didn't want to do was lose her forever.

I checked my watch and packed up my books and prepared to make my way out of the Spanish lab. I looked over at Jade again. I was about to send her a text but realized my battery had just died. *Damn*, I thought. *Okay, screw it. I'm just gonna go up*

to her and say something. Besides, it's not like she could have made a scene there in the lab.

"*¡Hola! ¿Cómo estas?*" I asked, walking up to her table.

"Um, *bien,*" she replied, looking up at me. "You are too funny."

"Aha, a smile, that's a good start. Look, don't worry, I'm not trying to sweat you or anything. I happened to be here too. I thought it was kind of crazy not to come over."

"No, no, it's all good." She smiled again. "Although, I was thinking you'd gotten lost or something. I don't think I've ever seen you in the Spanish lab." She laughed.

"So, what you workin' on?" I attempted to peek at her work.

"Hey!" she said, covering her computer screen.

"Oh, damn, my bad." I tossed my hands up in surrender. "I was just teasing."

"No, I'm sorry. Honestly, I'm not really working on Spanish. The library was too crowded so I came here. I'm working on an essay for this program I'm tryin' to get in to."

"Well, good luck," I said.

"Thanks. Oh, and thanks for that text last night, too. How's Whiteboy?"

"No problem. I'm glad your mom's better. Unfortunately, Whiteboy's not doing so well. He's in a coma," I said somberly.

"Oh, wow. I'm so sorry, Blue." She frowned. "Thankfully, you and Collin are there for him."

"Yeah, whatever," I said, twisting my mouth.

"I take it you guys didn't work things out."

"Nah, no chance of that. The damage can't be repaired at this point." Just the mention of Collin's name struck a nerve that made the blood race through my veins.

"Oh, wow, that's too bad. You guys have been friends way too long."

"Yeah, life is about change." There was an uncomfortable silence. "Um, so cool, I'd better go. And, um, by the way, I'm here for you if you ever need to talk. On the real, no strings, no hidden agendas, just a set of ears." I stood there with a stupid grin on my face. I'm sure she thought I looked like a fool.

"Thanks, um, well, I'd better get back to my essay." At that instant, I saw something in her eyes. It was like she wanted to tell me something. Maybe how much she missed me. Oh, hells yeah, she missed me! I could tell. Mission accomplished! Yes! I was the man. The ball was in Jade's court and I was going to let her have all the time she needed.

"Good luck with it. And don't forget what I said." I smiled. I was about to turn and walk away when a preppy-looking pretty-boy type approached. I hadn't seen him around SSH before.

"Hey there, you ready?" he said, setting a Starbucks cup down and putting his hand on Jade's shoulder. "I brought you a latte." We eyed each other up and down. On second thought, I wasn't going anywhere. Who *was* this fake punk-ass pseudo–Ralph Lauren busta? What straight guy wears a pastel pink shirt anyway?

"Thanks," Jade said, turning to him. "Wow, I wasn't expecting you for another twenty minutes."

"I finished class early and thought you might need a breather before we got started." He gave her a quick shoulder massage. What the hell! Okay, did my girl just forget I was standing here?

I cleared my throat loudly. "Errum, yo, Jade, who's your *friend*?"

"Oh, sorry, um, Blue, this is, um, Carlos." Jade could sense the awkwardness. I didn't give a damn about how uncomfortable she was. I wanted to know who this fool was who had just rolled up like some Hollywood star.

"Whassup?" I suspiciously glared.

"Carlos Reyes," he said with a smirk as he extended his hand. I didn't return the gesture.

"So, you new at SSH?" I asked, ignoring the fact that he was still waiting for me to shake his hand.

"Nah, bro, I go to HU," he said confidently. Oh, now he was trying to flex.

"Howard? That's cool. I'll be going there. So, um, you hang around high schools often?" I cracked, chuckling at his expense. This fool had triggered the wrong button. My temper had already been short lately. All I was sayin' was that fake-pimpin' better watch himself.

"Blue! That comment was uncool," Jade snapped.

"Yo, I'm just sayin', Jade, what's a college boy doin' around SSH?" My nostrils flared. I could feel my anger begin to boil in my veins. Homeboy better check himself in a serious way before I break him off.

"Jade, it's not a problem," he said with a laugh, throwing his hands in the air in surrender. "Yo, son, I ain't got no issue with you."

"I'm not your son, *son.*" I stepped back and puffed out my chest.

"My bad, that's how we do up in the Bronx," he said, sucking his teeth. Oh, hells yeah, it could go down right here if this clown felt like testing me.

"Blue, please! Carlos is a mentor in a program I'm trying to get into at Howard," she said, standing up, letting out a frustrated puff of air. Jade began stuffing her work into her tote bag. "I'm ready, Carlos." She picked up her Starbucks cup and walked away.

"Yo, my high school days are long gone, feel me, *son*?" he said, leaning into me. "I'm all about focusing on medical school. I got no time for beefin'. Besides, Jade's a beautiful young lady. I'd never want to disrespect her or another brotha." He winked and patted me on the back like I was some kind of f-ing puppy. This fool just made me look bad in front of Jade with his slick-mouthed collegiate act.

I wanted to punch something, but I couldn't let anybody see me sweat. I grabbed my backpack, stormed out of the lab, and made my way down the hall. I was dreading taking the Metro home, especially after that run-in. I put on my headphones, pressed play on my iPod, and slipped on my Ray-Ban aviators. My steps were in sync with the dope new track from Drake I had pumping. I was in a zone when all of a sudden my steps were intercepted by Collin slamming into me.

"What the . . ." I angrily shouted, ripping off my head-phones. Collin was pale and had a worried look on his face.

"We gotta get to the hospital right away. I just got a message about Whiteboy!"

"What happened?"

"I don't know for sure, but I think he's been trying to come out of the coma. The nurse said he's been showing signs all day."

"I don't have my car!"

"Screw it, just roll with me!" Collin motioned for me to follow him and we jetted off in the direction of the student parking lot.

CHAPTER FOURTEEN

WHITEBOY

I just wanna say my fault my bad
—Young Jeezy, "Might Just Blow That"

"Tommy? Tommy? Can you hear me?" I could hear a faint voice calling my name, but my eyes wouldn't open and I couldn't speak. I was trying to will my legs, my arms—something—to move.

"His blood pressure's going crazy. We've got to stabilize him." I heard another faint voice call out.

I was blinded by a bright light. *What's happening to me?* I thought. For an instant my Nana's face appeared. It was like I was dreaming *inside* my dream.

"I'm proud of you, Tommy." Nana smiled, reaching out to me. I was frozen with fear. Suddenly, she faded away, and I heard the sound of police sirens getting closer and closer, followed by the echoing sound of screeching tires. The sirens stopped and everything went silent.

I suddenly saw myself standing in the middle of my block, blood pouring down over my face. I had just relived the entire fight that night after leaving the club. I wiped the blood from my eyes, then stumbled to my car. I turned the ignition, slammed the car in drive, and sped off. The hospital was lit up in the distance, but it wasn't close enough. I blacked out.

I was jolted awake, my heart pounding so hard I thought it was going to jump out of my chest. A blurry image of Collin and Blue standing at the foot of the bed appeared. I was sweating like a fever had exploded all over my body. I couldn't figure out if I was still dreaming or if what I was seeing was real.

"He's back!" a nurse shouted. I was confused.

"Let's get his vitals stabilized!" another shouted. White coats surrounded me.

"Gentlemen, please step back while we work on your friend." Collin and Blue disappeared behind a wall of white coats.

"Tommy, if you can hear me, blink," a nurse commanded. I blinked. In fact, I blinked a gang of times. I answered all her questions, responding with blinks, nods, and finger pointing. I looked around the room and realized I was safe in the hospital.

"You went into shock and slipped into a short coma. We think you've come out of it just fine, but the neurologist will be in shortly to do a thorough check. Do you remember your friends Blue and Collin? Just give us a thumbs-up." She smiled, motioning for them to come closer. I gave them my middle finger, breaking up the seriousness in the room with laughter. You know I had to keep it real.

"Oh, he's definitely back!" Blue announced.

Several minutes later, I was still fading in and out of a semi-conscious state but slowly coming around. The beeping sound from the heart monitor machine had calmed to a normal rate. Collin and Blue were there holding me down on each side of my bed.

"You're quite a miracle, Tommy." One of the nurses smiled as she was filling out my chart. "You were in a coma for several days, but your brain and reflexes seem to be okay. The neurologist will be in shortly," she explained. "Guys, you can stick around for a bit, but then you'll have to leave. Just try to keep him calm." Blue and Collin nodded.

When the coast was clear, Blue leaned in closer. "Man, you okay?" he asked in a low voice. "Don't try to talk. I know you've got a lot of wires."

"Dude, you had us buggin' out for a minute," Collin added. "I'm glad you're back. We were scared." He gave a half smile. I tried to nod.

"Don't do all that, yo. We know you're good," Blue said, pulling up a seat.

"You're gonna pull through all this, man," Collin said.

I was somewhat confused. I remembered the wires in my

face, but when I looked down at my hand, I started to freak out. "Oooooooh," I moaned in anguish.

Collin panicked. "What's going on?"

"Yo, can't you see? He's upset about his hand," Blue shouted in a strained voice.

"Shut the hell up! You think I don't know that!" Collin fired back, doing his best to keep his voice down.

"Yo, on the real, you'd better fall back on all that, C!" Blue gave Collin a threatening look. I didn't know what to make out of what was going on, but I could tell something was definitely foul between the two of them.

"Mr. James, it's nice to see you back with us. I'm Dr. Chen, the head of neurology here at Holy Cross." The upbeat interruption from the doctor broke the tense vibe in the room. "Can you excuse us, gentlemen?" he said to Blue and Collin.

"Yeah, sure. Peace out, homie. I'll be back!" Blue said, throwing up the peace sign. "Oh, and, C, I'm cool on a ride home," he added, shooting a hard look in Collin's direction on his way out.

"Yeah, whatever," Collin said under his breath. "Sure, you'll be back. Anyway, I'm out too, Whiteboy, but keep your head up, dude. I started interning at my dad's office after school, so I won't be able to come by for a couple of days, but the hospital has my number. I'll be here in a heartbeat if you need something." He tossed his backpack over his shoulder and exited. Yeah, there was definitely something ill going on between the two of them, but I was dealing with my own issues right now.

As the doctor started to check me out, I could see my reflection in the mirror hanging over the sink on the other side of the room. The doctor carefully lifted up my injured arm and hand. Seeing all the tubes and wires and bandages triggered the frustration and anger to build inside me all over again. I couldn't look any longer. How was I gonna handle my business if I couldn't use that hand again? How was I gonna eat and survive without my art? I may as well not live. A stream of angry tears trickled down my face.

I wished I had died that night . . .

CHAPTER FIFTEEN

What up what's happenin'
All you haters can get at me
—T.I., "What Up What's Happenin'"

I spotted Collin checking out the menu in front of the Cyber Café as I was leaving last period. I thought about how messed up it was that we started arguing in front of Whiteboy the other day when he came out of the coma. I guess the adrenaline and tensions were running high for both of us.

I wanted to go up to him and say something just to clear the air. Not to have some big Kumbaya moment or anything, but I was thinking maybe we just need to call a truce, at least when we were around Whiteboy. Just then my phone alerted me of a text:

B @ THE CLUB FRI NITE MIDNITE ASK FOR BIG MIKE—RT

I double-checked the message to make sure I'd read it correctly. Yes! It was on. Things were finally happening. Tomorrow night I'd make my mark at Club Heat. That's whassup!

Collin was still standing by the café, and I was about to make a move in his direction when I saw Jade walking with a small group of friends. On second thought, Collin would have to wait. She and I had major unfinished business.

"Jade, yo, lemme holla at you for a minute!" I called out, running up to her and grabbing her arm.

"Blue!" she said, whipping around and yanking away. "Don't be grabbin' me like that! What do you want now?" she snapped, flipping her hair back.

"Yo, my bad putting my hands on you, that was disrespectful, but all that attitude ain't necessary. I just need to talk to you," I said, sliding between her and her two friends. They gave me all kinds of attitude, and huffs and puffs. I didn't care what they thought.

"How rude. You never cease to amaze me. I'm sorry, y'all," she said, turning to her friends. "I'll catch up in a few."

"Are you sure, Jade?" the short, dreaded one wearing glasses said, cutting her eyes at me.

"Jade, we can totally wait for you," the tall, blond one in braces added, standing next to her dreaded friend like a pitbull ready to attack. I wasn't even sweatin' the nerd crew.

"Do you mind, metal trap? I'm getting all kinds of feedback from your mouth." I smirked, throwing up my hand like a stop sign.

"Blue!" Jade punched me in the arm. "No, I'm good, girl. I'll meet you guys." She waited until they were out of earshot. "Blue, I tried to be nice when I asked you to leave me alone. And then I give you a tiny opening by responding to your text, and I was even cool about talking to you yesterday, but then you pull that stunt. You're pushing it."

"My bad. I just wanted to know what was up with that college dude. That cat's gonna catch a major problem if he ever steps to me and disrespects me again."

"Excuse me? First of all, none of your business! You really need to do something about your jealousy. I'm not your property, Blue! FYI, you need to quit sweatin' me about what I do and who I do it with! Look at your actions before you question mine! I'll say it again, you're *not* my boyfriend!" Then she stormed off.

It's one thing that me and Jade didn't work out, but then to have some cornball all up at SSH picking her up. It's like she was throwin' everything in my face. "Jade! Jade! Just make sure you tell your li'l friend to watch himself!" I yelled out to her. She fanned me off and kept walking. *To hell with her!* I said to myself, punching a nearby locker.

CHAPTER SIXTEEN

Sometimes love comes around and it knocks you down
Just get back up when it knocks you down
—Keri Hilson featuring Neyo. "Knock You Down"

All the essays were in and we'd find out today who was picked. We all took our seats. I was a bundle of nerves. Mr. Owens wasted no time.

"The essays you turned in determined your selection." My stomach did a series of backflips as he ran down the list of names. After four names, I still hadn't heard mine. I was preparing myself to be resolved with at least being in the running when all of a sudden Mr. Owens announced my name.

"Jade, you're not only our fifth selectee, but we saved the best for last, because you're also being recognized by the program because of your outstanding essay entitled 'Healthcare for All Children' and your vision to create pediatric clinics in urban cities all over the country."

Carlos was standing next to Mr. Owens, and both of them, along with the rest of the students in the room, broke into a rowdy round of applause. I almost fainted. "Jade, you will also be paired with Mr. Carlos Reyes for the entire program. He was so impressed by your essay and credentials he requested you as his mentee."

I was gushing with excitement and couldn't wait to get to the hospital to tell my mom. I was going to be living in the dorms on Howard's campus for a whole month, shadowing pre-med and med students at Howard's hospital, and we'd participate in seminars and symposiums about the latest medical breakthroughs. To top it off, we'd each get a $1,500 stipend. OMG! That was money that could go toward college.

I was so excited that I practically floated out of the building. In fact, I was oblivious to Carlos calling my name as I walked toward the Metro station until he started blowing his horn.

"Yo, do you always make brothas chase after you?" he teased, calling out to me from the open window of his fly-ass BMW 325i. Dang, he was fine, smart, and had a hot car.

"I'm sorry, I'm just excited about everything," I replied, slowing to a stop.

"You forgot," he coolly added, holding up a folder. "It's your essay."

"Wow. Sorry." I was slightly embarrassed. I quickly walked over to his car to relieve him of the folder.

"I'm looking forward." He flashed a million-dollar smile. "Hey, can I give you a ride?"

As tempting as *he*—I mean, *his* offer—was, I decided to pass. "No, thanks, maybe next time," I said, waving good-bye and continuing on my way. Oh yeah, he was definitely checking me out. I chuckled to myself at the thought of Blue being completely sick over himself if he had been there to see that. I giggled to myself as Carlos zoomed off, beeping his horn. I caught a glimpse of his smile one last time through his rearview mirror.

I was still flying high off my news when I breezed into Mama's room at the hospital.

"How are you feeling, Mama?" I whispered, gently kissing her on the forehead. "I've got good news," I said, practically bursting at the seams. I put my tote bag down and made an elaborate twirl, striking a serious *America's Next Top Model* pose. "You are looking at the top selectee for the upcoming Howard University summer program for high school honor students interested in medicine. Thank you very much!" I gleefully announced. "And, hold your applause. Mr. Owens said I wrote the best essay!" I let out a squeal.

"Oh, sweetface! This is the best news I've heard all day, all week, heck, all year," Mama gushed, applauding. "You make sure you copy that essay."

"Got it!" I said, holding it up.

"Well, I'll frame it as soon as I get outta this bed." Mama's eyes lit up and tears of joy poured down her face. "I'm crying because I'm happy. I know you're gonna be a great doctor one day."

"I'm gonna make you proud, I promise," I said, kissing her again.

"Baby, I'm proud every day." I pressed the button on her bed, gently lifting her up. I grabbed her hairbrush and started brushing her hair.

"And guess what," I said as her hair gently cascaded down her shoulders. "I get to live on Howard's campus and they give me a fifteen-hundred-dollar stipend."

"That's right on time, huh?" She smiled weakly. "Oh, sweet-face, that feels nice."

"Remember how I used to brush your hair all the time when I was a little girl?" I asked.

"I sure do, and you'd always get that brush tangled in it every time." We shared a laugh, and as the laughter trailed off, Mama grabbed my hand. "It was just me and my baby against the world. I would dress you up, tie pretty pink ribbons on your long braids, and we'd go out to the park," she said wistfully.

"Yeah, and that day you almost had to put the beat-down on that snotty white woman who was sitting next to us at the bus stop." I chuckled.

"The nerve of her! 'Miss, I think that's so nice of you to take that little black girl on park outings every week.' I was so angry. I looked her right in the eye and said, 'Isn't my little girl the prettiest chocolate-and-vanilla swirl you've ever seen!' That woman's mouth fell open. Some folks can be so ignorant, Jade, but it just made us stronger.

"Sweetface, you were my special gift from God," she said as I kissed her on the forehead. "I know things are tough right now, but I don't want you to worry. As soon as they get done with all these new tests and my treatment, I'll be able to get back to my old self and go back to my job at the nursing home, pick up some more hours."

Mama's a fighter. She's so strong and determined, even after battling cancer for the past year. It had been a tough haul, and she just never really bounced back all the way from having that double mastectomy. Right now the future just felt so uncertain. She had sacrificed so much for me.

"So what are they saying?" I yawned.

"Jade, look at you. You're exhausted. I hate that you have to work and go to school."

"Mama, it's cool."

"You'll have your whole life to work. Right now it's about studying and enjoying yourself. Speaking of enjoying yourself, I haven't heard you talk about that boy Blue lately."

"Humph, please!" I rolled my eyes. "There's nothing to talk about. He's desperate, jealous, and won't take no for an answer."

"That sounds like an awful lot to talk about. I thought you really liked him."

"Not anymore, and you know he's very selfish, Mama."

"Most men are."

"No, he's *really* selfish. Like all he talks about is the company he's going to have one day, Blue Up Productions this, Blue Up Productions that."

"Sounds like he's got ambition."

"I don't know about all that. I think his priorities are all messed up. Plus, I have a mentor for the program who's supercute and Blue had the nerve to get all up in my business in front of him. I'm like, whatever! It was totally embarrassing when that hoochified girl at his party was all over him. Bottom line, he thinks he's a playa, and I just decided to cut it off."

"That doesn't seem like the young man I met."

"Well, looks can be deceiving. I'm done with Blue Reynolds."

"Jade, I know that you can shut people off sometimes, people who really care about you. It doesn't sound like you're being very fair, sweetface. I think this kid Blue is a nice guy."

"Mama, how do you know that?" I smirked.

"I saw it in his eyes. He's a dreamer. I think we just have a thing for dreamers. You get that from me." Suddenly she winced in pain.

"Mama, are you okay?"

"I'd better rest. I'm gonna be okay, promise, sweetface," she said, placing her hand on my cheek. "Jade, we're gonna get through this together."

"We've always been a team, Mama." I smiled.

"Listen, they ran some new tests and the news might not be so good, but you've got to promise me that you'll be strong."

"I promise, Mama," I said, wrapping my arms around her as she drifted off to sleep.

It's funny, it really had always been just my mom and me. She'd had to be the mother and the father in our household. She was my rock, and I wasn't going to disappoint her. I knew that as soon as she was better, our bills would be paid on time and life would be all good again. In the meantime, I had to do what I had to do to hold things down.

CHAPTER SEVENTEEN

BLUE

Free to see
From the penitentiary in our mind
—Citizen Cope, "Penitentiary"

I'd been putting in serious work at school and I had one more day to go before my big night working Club Heat. I stopped in the library to pick up a book, and when I opened my notebook to check something, the old flyer from my first party at Club Toast slipped out. I picked it up off the floor and examined it closely. The artwork was incredible, all due to Whiteboy's genius. He mixed graffiti with cool graphics, and there was a photo of me and Collin at the center. Those were definitely happier times.

My conscience was getting to me again. I still felt mad guilty about me and Collin arguing in front of Whiteboy, and I knew I hadn't really been there for him. I'll give Collin his props. He had stepped up big-time on the friend tip. I guess I'd come up short in that department throughout the entire situation with Whiteboy. It was time for me to do the right thing and go see him. I quickly stuffed the flyer back in my notebook, grabbed the book I needed, and called Moms to get an okay to make a pit stop at the hospital before heading home.

When I arrived at the hospital, I was surprised to see Whiteboy sitting up. I poked my head in his room. He was alone. Whiteboy was expressionless, using his left hand to change channels with the remote. His injured hand was in a cast and propped up in what appeared to be a new sling. He was actually looking much better than the last time I saw him. His face was still wired, but the bruises were fading.

"Ay, yo! What's good!" Whiteboy looked surprised to see me. "I know you can't talk and stuff, but I wanted to come by and check you out." I nervously slid a chair up next to his bed. "Plus, tell you I was sorry, um, for how I acted the last time I was here. You know, beefin' with C and all."

"Mmmmm, huh." Whiteboy nodded and tried to talk, but gave up and picked up the pen and paper sitting on his tray. He scribbled a message slowly:

AIN'T SEEN U N A WHILE

"Sorry about that. I've just been real busy." He nodded, but I could tell he probably thought my excuse was lame. "Anyway, man, you really scared me for a minute when you were in that coma," I said. Whiteboy nodded again, but this time his reaction was more of an assuring one. Letting me know that he was okay now. "But yo, on a funny note, you do kinda look like Kanye did in that 'Through the Wire' video," I lightheartedly joked, trying to cheer him up. Whiteboy flashed me his left-hand middle finger. "Yeah, I got love for you too! I see you're definitely getting back to normal now."

His expression turned serious as he reached for the pen and pad and scribbled out another note.

YO SORRY ABOUT THE PARTY AND THE FIGHT

"Whiteboy, the most important thing is that you're alive. That's over. I'm just glad you're alive."

I'M A SOLDIER

He scratched out furiously, letting out a moan from a sharp pain.

"Chill, dude!" I was startled and unsure what to do. He took a deep breath, regained control over the pain, and scratched out another message.

SO WHY AIN'T C WIT U

"Not sure. I haven't talked to him."

STOP PLAYIN

I looked at his note and I knew I had to tell him the truth. I couldn't front like everything was okay between me and Collin. "I'll be honest, things just aren't very cool right now between us. They haven't been. The whole Blue Up thing didn't work out," I said, watching Whiteboy painfully shake his head. "But hey, the good news is, I've been busy tryin' to rebuild," I said cheerfully. "I'm actually Rico Tate's new protégé. Tomorrow's my first night on the job, so I'm gonna leave soon. I've gotta get a ton of homework done so I can be ready," I said while he scratched out another note.

I MESSD UP YO

He frowned.

I KNOW IT'S MY FAULT

"C'mon, let it go. There are a lot of things between me and Collin that go deep, and that don't have nothin' to do with you."

He made an angry grunting sound, took a long pause, and continued writing.

BULLSHIT B!

He wrote, then gave up, dropped the pen, let out another moan, and reached for his injured hand with his other one.

"Aw, man, you're in a lot of pain," I said, panicked, looking for the nurse call button. "Yo, I know, but they're gonna fix you up good and it'll be like brand-new." Whiteboy gave me a pained look like I had just given him the biggest line of crap ever.

I found the button and pressed it repeatedly.

"Look, I mainly wanted to come by and apologize for the other day. You didn't deserve that." Whiteboy refused to look at me. My efforts were in vain.

Just then the nurse came in. "Sorry, but it's time for him to get his pain medicine," she said, hurriedly filling a syringe with a cloudy fluid and injecting it into his IV. "You need your rest, Mr. James. Sir, I'm sorry but you'll have to leave now."

"Look, I'm just gonna go. I hope I didn't upset you by coming here." I felt like crap. Maybe this was a mistake. "Just know I got your back no matter what, yo." Whiteboy suddenly turned toward me and weakly gave me the peace sign, signaling that I was dismissed.

CHAPTER EIGHTEEN

MAMIE

**I'm scared to start cause I'm scared I'll quit
—Jazmine Sullivan, "Fear"**

I raced into work and gave a round of girlfriend smooches to my girl Jade.

"Sorry I'm late," I said, quickly putting on my apron. "What's up!"

"Oh, girl, looking at this ka-razee message from that guy Carlos," Jade said, scrolling through her messages.

"The college guy. OMG! You got a college man?"

"Slow your roll! No, he's my *mentor*," Jade insisted. "And do not tell your boy Collin my business. I'm not trying to have psycho Blue in my mix, which ain't a mix to get into 'cause there's nothing going on between me and the guy."

"Girl, don't worry, your secret's safe. Plus, him and Blue

don't even speak. Anyway, mentor, smentor! Who you foolin'? He tryin' to get at you, ain't he?"

"No," Jade replied in disbelief. "Although, he did ask me to go to lunch or dinner one day."

"Oooh, you should go. So what? You're a free bird."

"I dunno, maybe."

"You've got my vote. He's fine *and* has a BMW. Uh, hello, no-brainer!" We high-fived. "So how's your moms?" I asked, touching her shoulder.

"She's hanging in there," she replied, letting out a deep breath and putting her phone away. "It's just that for the past week they've been running crazy tests. They say her white blood count is really high. I don't know. I've never prayed so much in my life. Anyway, between here, the hospital, and homework, I'm burning the candle at both ends and in the middle."

"Don't even mention homework to me. That's a joke. I'm so over school," Mamie said with a flippant attitude.

"Girl, you sound crazy!"

"I'm serious. The other day Mr. Jones read me my last rites."

"What?" Jade chuckled.

"I'm basically on academic probation."

"Hello! That means you'd better get your act together." Jade scooped up a steamy plate of veggie pasta.

"Jade, you know I've got more important things to worry about."

"Like what?" She put her free hand on her hip.

"Like I came up with a beat that's so dope for Tre. I'm gonna lay it down when we go in the studio tomorrow night, girlie!" We high-fived. "Our mix CD is going to take us to the next level. I'm not trippin' off Mr. Jones or my aunt Deb, who freaked out about this whole probation thing he just hit me with. I'm actually thinking more about dropping out," I said matter-of-factly.

"Girl, are you crazy!" Jade screeched.

"Look, Jade, there's a lot that's been going on over the past few weeks. My aunt even kicked me out. But I'm cool. I've been staying with Collin. Is that crazy, or what?"

"What! Why didn't you tell me?"

"Because you've got enough crap in your life. I'm fine. His dad's never there and the house is so big he'd never know."

"Okay, okay, this is way too much info. I'm hyped about the studio thingy, but pissed off about the school situation and your aunt's house, but hold that thought. I've gotta drop off! I'll be back." She whisked away the plate of food.

I inconspicuously slipped on my earphones and pulled out the tray of empty salt and pepper shakers and started to fill them. I slipped into a zone.

"Mamie!" Jade tugged, startling me. "Are you on drugs or something? You can't quit school. You can't get anywhere in life without education, and you can't live on your own."

"Why not? I've been living on my own forever," I replied nonchalantly.

"My point is you need to get serious about school. And

what about college? Look, if nothing else, you've gotta have a high school diploma to function in this world."

"My beats and talent are all the diploma or degree I need, chickie. I don't need the pressure of school," I said, screwing the top back on one of the salt shakers.

"Mamie, think about what you're saying."

"I have already."

"Excuse me, this is not social hour!" our boss Miss Shante snapped as she peeked around the corner. "Back to work, chickens!" We quickly pretended to be hard at work. When the coast was clear we resumed our conversation.

"Hello? I asked you a question. What are you going to do?"

"If I don't have my music, I ain't got nothing. Bottom line, school ain't for everybody and it ain't a priority. I just gotta do me, and if that means not going to school, just tell me you'll still be my girl." I held out my pinkie finger.

"Fly-girl honor!" Jade reluctantly held out her pinkie, and we sealed the deal by locking fingers. "I love you," she said, hugging me. "I don't like what you're doing, but I love you. Look, I gotta go. I'm sleeping at the hospital tonight." We gave each other a good-bye round of girlfriend smooches.

CHAPTER NINETEEN

BLUE

I thought I told you Imma star
You see the ice? You see the cars?
—Jeremih, "Imma Star (Everywhere We Are)"

**RIGHT TRAK STUDIO 2NITE @ 10 . . . DJ ILL MAMA
GOT THAT FI-YAH TO TAKE U HI-YAH IT'S ON!**

Tonight was the night! And it was definitely on. It's true when it rains, it monsoons! Not only was I about to be representin' at the club tonight as Rico Tate's protégé, but Mamie and Tre were going into the studio. Soon I was going to have their first mix CD to show off. I had to be on point for a jam-packed agenda.

I put everything out of my mind—Jade and her obvious lies, my beef with Collin, even Whiteboy flippin' on me at the hospital. In less than two hours my life was going to start

changing for real. I was on my way to super mogul/super manager sooner than I imagined! I heard a car pull into the driveway and peeked out my bedroom window. Aw, hells no!

My pops had returned a day early from his New York trip. This was definitely throwing a wrench in my plans. *Okay, okay, think fast, Blue. Don't panic*, I told myself.

"Blue, your father's home, come on down for dinner!" Moms yelled.

I took a deep breath. Mom was always in bed by nine. Dad usually around ten, give or take a few minutes. I just had to adjust my plan. I couldn't be late for the club. So I'd have to make the studio stop more of an in-and-out deal. Bet! I took another deep breath before heading downstairs for dinner.

There was barely any conversation during dinner. I could deal with a lot, but when your father won't even look at you, it cuts deep. My mother was still trying to get him to soften up.

"Blue, why don't you give your dad an update on school."

"Oh, yeah, I've been really putting in some good study time."

"So when am I going to see some grades? Until you have something to show me, there's not a lot we need to be discussing."

"I've got a big history test coming up next week and I'm turning in an English paper tomorrow, oh, and it looks like I should ace my Spanish test."

"I'm about results and the facts. Oh, and even though your friend is in the hospital, just remember you've got responsibilities around here. This is a crucial time for you. Excuse me, I'm going to catch the news," he grumbled, pushing back from the table. He cleared his plate and retired to the family room.

It was clear that the only way I was going to get back in his good graces was to give him the proof. Until then, I'd have to tough out living in this freakin' prison of a home. In the meantime, it was all about my exit plan tonight.

By ten o'clock, my father had passed out from exhaustion and a couple of glasses of red wine. My mom had fallen asleep reading in bed. It was time to get it poppin'. I made sure to pick out an outfit that would let everyone know I was the new flava. Rico was probably going to have some special VIP duties for me. I wanted to look the part.

I put on my fresh Adidas, my Rock & Republic jeans, and an Ed Hardy hoodie over a white tee. As I gave myself the once-over in the mirror, I slipped on a pair of aviator shades. I was definitely looking the part of a minimogul. I was good to go. I quietly locked my bedroom door and grabbed the spare set of keys to Mom's SUV I had stashed under my mattress.

I quietly climbed out my bedroom window. Our house was a bi level, but luckily my room faced the side of the house, and right below my window was an awning. I made my escape to the car, jumped in, slid the gearshift into reverse, and coasted down the block in neutral. Once I was in the clear, I hit the ignition, slammed the car in drive, and sped off. First stop, Right Trak.

Mamie and Tre were already hard at work when I arrived at the studio. I slid in just as Tre was putting his headphones on in the booth. Miles gave me a pound. I gave a nod to Mamie, who was sitting next to Loc behind the board. When her track came on it was so fire we all immediately started bobbing our heads. Mamie's tracks were even more blazin' than before.

"Yeah, yeah, yeah, yeah. It's the young one comin' back for anotha son-day. It's a new day, a grab your mind and get schooled day. I'm not here to spit about money and chicks and all that superficial ***, I'm here to open your mind, take you on a head trip with some real ***. It's about havin' that faith to make it your own way no matter what they say. Keep it legit and stick wit that gift. The fame and money will always be 'round. Young Tre on the mic can't hold me down!"

"I'm just warming up, B!" he said, stepping out of the booth. "Nice gear!" He gave me a pound.

"Yeah, you know how I do. I'm headed to the club from here. My first night!" I was definitely feelin' like a major mover and shaker.

"Make those connections. We comin' with heat this time!" Tre added before dashing back into the booth.

"We'll be working all night to get this mix CD done," Mamie called out from the board area. She was hard at work like she was born to produce. "We should have some early copies as soon as tomorrow."

"Come by and scoop some copies," Miles added.

"Bet!" I said, making my good-bye rounds. If the mix CD was half as hot as what they'd got poppin' off in the studio tonight, we were about to all be outta here!

When I pulled up in front of Club Heat, it was even more of a zoo than when I was there last. The music was incredible. Hip-hop on one level, R & B on another, jazz in an uber-VIP room, and then go-go pumping out of yet another VIP room. I had died and gone to club heaven. I quickly parked the car in the back lot and raced to the front door. A bouncer instructed me to wait inside the front office.

I must've stood in that tiny, windowless front office for at least thirty minutes before anyone came to get me. I was hoping they hadn't forgotten I was in there. Although I was clueless, I was still hyped just to be there. The boom from the club speakers had the whole place shaking. I couldn't wait to work the room. Just then there was a loud knock at the door. The door opened, revealing a dude about the size of a refrigerator.

"You the new guy?" this cat about six-four asked. "You need to take all that other stuff off, pimpin'. Cleanup crew wears all black. We'll let you slide with the blue jeans tonight, but from here on out, black pants or black jeans only." He tossed me a black shirt. "Oh, and you might want to take the shades off, playa." He laughed, adding a mop and bucket to my revamped club attire. "If you have any questions, everybody calls me Big Mike."

I was given a laundry list of crap-level chores. First stop, bathroom duty. I knew guys were bad, but the ladies' room was just plain *nasty*! I put the BATHROOM CLOSED sign in front of the door and went to work. There were balled-up paper towels everywhere. Man, had these honeys heard of a thing called a trash can, and yo, didn't they learn when they were like two that you're supposed to *flush* a toilet after you pee in it? I angrily flushed a toilet stuffed with mounds of toilet paper.

"Um, hello! We gotta come in there, can you hurry up!" I turned around at the sound of an irate patron's voice. My mouth fell open. Babygirl was bangin'. I was stuck on her perfectly bronze legs and the sequined mini that framed her perfect *asset,* if you know what I mean. Her girl looked queasy and was hanging on to her like a ragdoll.

"What are you, stupid or somethin'? How about you take a picture? It'll last longer!" she ordered, charging into the bathroom with her drunk friend, who was kinda hot too. "Excuse me!" she said, pushing past me with her staggering friend. And then the drunk did the ultimate and threw up all over the stall floor. Ewww! There went my fantasy. This was gonna be a *long* night. I grabbed the mop and went to work.

I finally got the ladies' room up and running again and didn't even have a chance to catch my breath before I was being ordered to go up to the third-level bathrooms and clean them. I must've done enough cardio for the rest of the year. It was bad enough I was the janitor, but for the next hour I shared the dual title of trash specialist, carting large black bags of stinking, leaking garbage to the alley.

"Yo, Big Mike," I called out as I re-entered the club from the alley, where I had just dumped what I hoped was my last load of trash. He was standing near the deejay booth with two other security guys. "Am I going to just clean the bathrooms and take out the trash for the rest of the night?" I said in disgust.

"My bad, I forgot all about you, li'l homie." He chuckled. Guffaws broke out from the other cats. "Go tell Ricardo in the VIP kitchen that you're his replacement. After you take care of things, you can burn out."

Yeah, that's what I'm talkin' about, a familiar word in my vocabulary—VIP. However, when I entered the VIP kitchen, I got the opposite surprise. A tatted up dishwasher pointed Ricardo out to me. He was wearing all black and holding a clipboard. He looked to be writing down important information.

"Yo, Big Mike said I'm your replacement," I said confidently.

"Cool, grab that mop over there. Make sure you soap the floor down good and then give it another once-over." I stood there in yet another moment of shock. I thought I'd be relieving him, as in possibly being in the company of celebrities in the house tonight, or at *least* scribbling on that pad of paper like he was doing. "Yo, homie?" he snapped, pointing to the mop before exiting.

Ain't this about some straight-up bs, I thought, grabbing the mop and angrily slam-dunking it into the bucket of dirty, sudsy water. This was definitely *not* what I had in mind. I was *supposed* to be Rico's protégé.

CHAPTER TWENTY

Ain't nobody dope as me I'm just so fresh so clean
—OutKast, "So Fresh, So Clean"

INTRODUCING YOUNG TRE . . .
ANACOSTIA'S FINEST SPITS THE TRUTH!!!

After church, I blasted out a mass text and posted it on my Facebook page. Life was sweet, because Mamie was about to deliver copies of my first mix CD. which were printed and packaged with Whiteboy's dope artwork. I had a little home-work to get out the way, but it was hard to concentrate. I was preoccupied thinking about the mix CD's arrival. Plus, I hated calculus.

I sat down at my desk and opened my math book to the

problem I was stuck on. I never struggled with any of my classes, but this one was tough.

"Whassup, cuz? You gotta lay off the books. It's Sunday, chill day. I'm psyched about the mix," Miles said, entering the room.

"I know, dude. I gotta finish this or nobody's mix is gonna matter."

"Mamie's gonna be here in about an hour, ain't she?" Miles plopped down on his bed and began spitting one of my verses from the recording session.

"Yo, I'm glad you jockin' me, but it's a distraction."

"My bad, but I'm bored."

"So what!" I started reviewing the problem I had been stuck on. "Hmmm, problem y equals, urgh! I keep messing this up!" I shouted out of frustration.

"What is it?"

"Yeah, okay, sure." I smirked.

"Try me," he said, tossing his football in the air and catching it.

"Okay, true or false. The two functions of f and g defined by $f(x) = 3x + 3$ for x real and $g(t) = 3t + 3$ for t real and positive are equal? Your go, playa!"

"That's easy. False. Two functions are equal if their rules are equal and their domains are the same," he said confidently.

"Dog, how did you get that! Miles, you're crazy smart!" I said, shocked.

"I never said I wasn't. Look, I promise to help you with this calculus stuff if you promise *not* to do anymore homework today."

"That's whassup!" We high-fived and got down to business.

An hour later my calculus homework was done and checked. I couldn't believe Miles had come through like a true mathematician.

"I got one question, Miles," I said, putting my books away. "Why are you pretending to everyone like you aren't smart?"

"I'm not pretending anything. Look, cuz, back home calculus doesn't get you props in the hood. Anyway, let's be out. Your girl Mamie will be here any minute." Miles was good at changing the subject. I'd let him slide for now, but his logic was just plain illogical to me. He needed to face the fact that he wasn't in Cali anymore.

"Whassup, supastar?" Mamie said, walking up my front steps holding a box of CDs. "I'm so proud of our first full-length mix, Tre." She handed me the box.

"You look fly," I said, checking her out from head to toe. She looked good too, rockin' her skinny jeans, a sexy tank top, and a leather bomber. She was keepin' it extra fresh with a pair of colorful Nike Air Force 1's. Blue exited the car right behind her.

"Thanks." She smiled.

"Yeah, real fly," Miles said with a wink. I hated how he jocked Mamie every time she came around.

"Yo, Miles, give Mamie some air." I snapped.

"Why, Tre, you afraid of the competition?" Miles snickered.

"Okay, boys, I'm on sensory overload!" Mamie said, cutting us both off. "Can we just focus on the CD, please, thank you?" I gave Miles a look.

"Whassup, Blue!" I called out as he approached.

"Yo, y'all got the *ish*! The CD is fire!" Blue said, giving me and Miles a pound.

"Anyway, Blue, how'd last night go?"

"Oh, the club?" Blue looked surprised I'd asked. "Oh, yeah, it was cool, real cool."

"Well, now you got the goods to make Rico really pay attention," I said, giving Mamie a high five.

"Yeah, well, they're real busy; it might take me a little longer than I thought, but I'm on it!" He winked.

"So how'd you swing getting out the house today?" Miles asked, shooting a wink right back at me.

"Let's just say I'm creative with my words. Nah, I'm supposed to be at the library. Forget all that, though, how does it feel to have your first official mix CD?" Blue shouted.

"Great!" I replied.

"So, you happy?" Mamie asked, flashing a coy grin.

"I'm happy, proud, ecstatic, hyped! Should I go on?" I said, placing the box down and holding up one of the mix CDs.

"No, silly!" Mamie said, giving a sexy giggle.

"Well, I think it's hot like you," he said, grabbing her hand and kissing it.

"Chill, Miles, this is about business," I snapped.

"Aw, I see I'd better chill; cuz is gettin' territorial," Miles joked, giving Blue a pound.

"Whatever, man. Anyway, you out, Mamie?" I said, shifting my attention back to her.

"Yeah, I gotta hit that work grind."

"What about you, Blue?" Miles asked.

"I rode over with Mamie, but I may stick around," he said, examining the artwork on the CD. "But while I have everyone here, I've got something to say, errum," he said, clearing his throat. "I just wanna say thanks to Young Tre and DJ Ill Mama, and Miles too. I appreciate you guys giving me another chance and rollin' the dice. It hasn't been easy, but you got hotness here." He raised the CD in the air. "I promise to make some power player pay attention!"

"Here, here!" We all cheered. Mamie and I noticed Blue's sudden change in emotion as he stared at the CD again.

"Blue, you okay?" Mamie asked.

"I'm good, just checkin' out Whiteboy's artwork. I guess it just hit me how bad he is. You know, that and the fact that I feel like the last guy standing in my crew."

"Yo, why don't you and Collin just squash your beef?" I asked. "I mean, is it really worth it?" I sat down on the steps.

"I probably shouldn't say this, but I think Collin's been bummed too. He also said Whiteboy's really depressed."

"I'm gonna get by there. I've just been . . ." Blue said.

"Busy?" Mamie said with a raised eyebrow.

"Yo, Blue, we've all been busy, but make time for your boy. That's real," I added.

"Okay, enough of the sad stuff, today's an amazing day! I'm out! Gotta get to work. Hopefully, these will get you started, Tre," Mamie said, and gave me another hug. "I'm having some more printed up! Represent for us!" she said, dashing off and jumping in her car. My eyes followed her as she pulled off.

"You feelin' babygirl, huh?" Miles said to me, giving Blue a look.

"You and Mamie? For real?" Blue said with shock. "I mean, she's fine. I thought you like the more scholarly types."

"Nah, I mean, I like all types. She's cool. But it's all business. How did we get on that topic, anyway? Let's roll," I said, changing the subject.

"I'll leave that one alone," Blue said.

"Me too. Cuz be gettin' all sensitive," Miles joked, giving Blue a pound.

"Damn, is gettin' with honeys all you fools think about?" I said.

"Somethin' like that!" Miles gave Blue another pound. We broke into laughter.

"Back to my mix—you think it's gonna sell, Blue? You think we can get somethin' poppin'? I got folks comin' after me hard."

"I know, but I'm down and I'm not going to bail on you and Mamie again. I think it's dope!" Blue said. "Seriously, you could go to the top with this one."

Just holding the CD in my hands felt good. Me, Miles, and Blue were on the serious hustle, and I was ready to celebrate on the block.

"You did it, cuz," Miles said, patting me on the back as we made our way down the street.

"Let's get this paper!" I boasted.

"Well said, family!" Miles gave me a high five.

My man Sauce was the first to hand over his five dollars. His endorsement was all the rest of the hood needed. He gave the official wave for the line to start behind him. People hanging out on their porches and even the heads chillin' on the corner got in line to buy a copy of the fresh new sound from yours truly and DJ Ill Mama.

I will give it to Miles. He kept the flow organized and the line orderly. Between him and Blue, and Whiteboy's artwork, I looked like a ready-made multiplatinum hoodstar. I was sure the fellas flipped over the shot of Mamie in stilettos behind the turntables. Cats were asking who she was, and I felt myself actually getting jealous.

"Sold out!" Blue announced.

"We only had twenty-five copies with us, but it was all good because the demand had exceeded our supply for the day," Miles said. "We've gotta get some more copies made. So we can *really* get paid!"

"Dude, we made one twenty-five in just twenty-five minutes!" I said.

"Cuz, five dollars a minute is better than minimum wage! I think I might like it here in DC after all."

After that we decided to just chill and hang out. Miles was goofing around, tossing up his football with Blue. Miles had met practically everyone in the neighborhood. I thought he was starting to like it here in DC. The sun was out, and in the infamous words of the legendary Ice Cube, Today was a good day! Yessir!

Sauce pumped the mix CD on his boom box, old-school style.

"Tre, this music is incredible. The world needs to hear it, young bro," Sauce said.

"Yeah, I know, that's why I'm on the grind."

"I told him he could kill those wannabe MCs on *106 and Park*," Miles added. "We're gonna have more copies of his mix for sale soon too." He winked, tossing the ball to me.

"I don't know. Some of those cats are really talented on Freestyle Fridays," I said, catching the ball.

"Tre, Miles is right. You're doper than most of the cats who win!" Blue added.

"Cuz, it's just like me and football. I know I'm one of the best running backs in Long Beach in my division. I believe it in here," he said, pointing to his chest. "When you got it in there, no one can fade you."

"Whatever, man!" Scottie, the younger brother to this wild hood named Vaughn, snickered. Scottie was always talking trash. "Lookin' like Ricky from Boyz n da Hood!" Laughter erupted.

"I see you got jokes, playa!" Miles cocked his head to the side. What I will say about Miles is that he doesn't back down from anybody. Maybe it's that Cali attitude.

"Yo, young, I'm the fastest runner *and* the best linebacker at Anacostia High, and no running back can elude me," Scottie said, high-fiving the other guys in the crowd.

"Do I hear a challenge?" Blue announced.

"Word? Well, let's put some money on your speed." Miles gave me and Blue a pound. I knew my cousin was about to straight hustle these fools and they didn't know it. I smiled.

"I got ten on my cousin!" I said.

"I got ten on Miles too!" Blue pulled out a ten. The older guys in the crowd, even Scottie's big brother, Vaughn, tossed their tens in. The pot had a good sixty bucks in it.

We all moved to the end of the block and I called out, "On your mark, get set, go!" Scottie was fast, but he was no match for Miles, who took that sprint easily.

"Yeah, whatever, man. I don't care how fast you are," he

panted. "If you get on the football field, I'll destroy you. Let's double the pot," he said, eyeing his brother.

"I got you," Vaughn called out.

"Check this out, pimpin'. Let's do some one-on-one, linebacker versus running back," Miles proposed, tossing his ball in the air.

"I don't know about that, Scottie. My cousin's pretty tight," I said, giving Miles a pound. "Let's take it to the park!"

Everyone jogged over to nearby Fort Dupont Park. It was on! As soon as Miles hit the grass, he was no joke. I had heard Sweets brag about how good he was, and his mom always sent us pictures of him and his team; however, his game was beyond what I expected. Miles's skills were tight! He had speed, agility, and smarts on the field. Scottie was known around here as the best, but he was no match for Miles.

"Yo, this was a crazy day, Tre. I'm out!" Blue said, giving me a pound. "Miles, you got mad skills on the field. You gotta try out for my boy Chuck's football league!"

"Say the word!" Miles called out as Blue headed toward the Metro.

When Blue left we headed home, but not before getting in a few more digs to Scottie, who was puffing up like he was about to cry.

"Yo, Scottie, Miles juked the shit out of you like three times when he ran you over on that fourth attempt. He made you look mad silly!" Sauce and some of the other older guys teased to the point that Scottie wanted to fight.

"Watch yourself, young!" Scottie shouted like a mad little kid ready to take his ball and go home.

"No, pardner, you watch them calories." Miles patted his stomach. "You got a good twenty-five on me, playa!" Everyone broke out into laughter all over again.

CHAPTER TWENTY-ONE

BLUE

You think the way you live's okay
You think posing will save the day
—N.E.R.D, "Rock Star"

YO, BE @ THE CLUB 2NITE SAME TIME—BIG MIKE

Then I was hit with another text. This time from Tre:

**YO WHASSUP? YOU WORKIN' THE CLUB 2NITE?
PUSH THAT MIX PLAYA! WE'RE COUNTIN' ON U**

I let out an exasperated sigh. He had no idea what an uphill battle I was in the middle of. I quickly typed back:

I'M ON IT . . . STAY TUNED

Now if I could only get off janitorial duty.

I was just about to put my phone away when it buzzed again. It was Chuck:

WHAT'S GOING ON WITH YOU? YOU NEVER GOT BACK TO ME ON WHEN YOU WERE COMING TO THE CENTER TO WORK WITH THE KIDS

My phone was blowin' up, and Chuck had really killed my vibe with all that volunteering stuff. I had enough pressure to get the CD heard. I swore I was gonna get back to him. I hated that I'd fallen through on my promise to him, but right now there was just too much going on. I *promised* I was going to make time for the center real soon. I didn't want to totally dis him, so I sent him another stall message:

POPS STILL HAS ME ON LOCKDOWN . . . REAL SOON—PEACE B

I shut my phone down and got back to my homework. I had to knock out everything before going to the club. I was still tired from finishing at three this morning. I knew that after two nights back-to-back I wouldn't have the brainpower to finish tomorrow. Plus, I was sure Moms was gonna be on me about going to church.

I scrolled through my e-mails and opened the message from my Spanish teacher. It was a progress note and my recent test scores. I held my breath as I opened it. When I clicked on the attachment and saw the A, I practically leaped for joy. Maybe now I could get my dad off my back.

I hurried and printed it out and shut down my computer, racing downstairs to my mother, who was reading a magazine in the living room.

"Hey, Mom, check this out." I handed her the printout as soon as I walked into the living room.

"Wow, an A! Nice work, Blue. It's been a while." She smiled.

"I just printed it out. You know how I do! Just a li'l somethin' somethin'," I bragged. "How's Dad's mood? I wanna show him, but what do you think?"

"I think now's a good time." She winked.

I gathered my courage and headed into the family room, where Dad was casually looking over some files and scrolling through his BlackBerry. He seemed to be somewhat relaxed.

"Hey, Dad, can I join you?" He nodded. "How's work?" I said, trying to break the ice, sitting down on the sofa.

"You never ask me about work. What brings that on?" He gave me a surprised look. "But since you did, I'm going to court on Monday with a tricky discrimination case. But I think we've got a great shot at winning. Thanks for asking." He gave a half smile.

"I'm really interested, Dad. And by the way, it's not so bad spending a weekend at home with your parents," I said, checking the time on my phone on the sly.

"So you got any grades to show me yet?" My dad replied flatly.

"Actually, I do. Bam!" I beamed, flashing him my Spanish exam. He grabbed his reading glasses off the coffee table, gave the paper a once-over, then did a double take.

"This is what you should've been doing all along." He nonchalantly put his glasses back on the table.

I felt defeated. I got up to exit.

"By the way, is your friend Whiteboy better?" My father's words stopped me in my tracks.

"Yeah, he's outta the coma," I said, turning back around. "But it's still gonna be a long road. He's got a broken jaw and his hand is pretty messed up. The rest is just minor stuff."

"Tell him we're pullin' for him to get better."

"Definitely."

"How's Collin doing?"

"We're not really communicating much right now."

"That's too bad. This hasn't been a good time for any of us, but remember, real friendship doesn't come along very often. You both share responsibility in what happened."

"Yeah, I hear you, but right now talking doesn't seem like much of an option. Anyway, I'm gonna get a little more studying in before turning in," I said, quickly getting off that subject.

"So early?"

"Yeah, gotta store up energy to keep makin' those A's, right?"

"I like your thinking. Good night, son. Oh, and as far as

that Spanish grade, I'm glad you're turning things around, but you've still got a lot to do. It's all about staying diligent. Okay?" I felt like there had been a semi-breakthrough between me and my dad. It gave me hope.

"Dad, I know I really disappointed you," I said, lowering my head and letting out a sigh. "And until I can really show you the change I've made in black and white, my words aren't going to mean a lot. But I'm going to do everything I can to win your trust back."

"Son, it's been a long few weeks for all of us, but I still have faith in you." He gave me a reassuring nod.

I exited the room, but peeked back in on the sly. I could see him yawn as he put his file away, hit the power on the remote, and reclined in his chair. That chair had magic knockout powers. He was about to be out like a light, *and* he was sipping on some red wine. That was the sign I needed. He'd be going to bed soon. I quietly tiptoed back to my room and closed the door.

By ten fifteen I could hear my parents' synchronized snores. Like clockwork, Mom and Dad were asleep. I slipped on my black gear and prepared to make my escape. I climbed out of my bedroom window, hopped in Mom's SUV, coasted in neutral down the block, revved up the engine, and was off to the club, blasting Jay-Z's "Dirt Off Your Shoulders."

The line was around the block when I pulled up to the club. The bouncers in front of the VIP line were dressed in black suits and wearing headsets. I was steaming with envy, dressed in black jeans and a T-shirt. I sucked up my pride, parked, and made it inside right on time. Rico gave me a reality check, that's for sure.

I reported in to Big Mike and got busy on bathroom duty. After an hour of what had quickly become routine, I was reassigned to mule duty. That meant carrying trays of glasses, water, and basically anything that weighed at least a ton up and down three levels in the biggest club in DC. For the next hour I ran up and down the steps, collecting empty glasses from each level. I must've carried over a hundred glasses. Some protégé I was.

I decided to take a breather after about ten trips up and down the stairwell. Level two was crazy tonight. DJ Drama, T.I.'s deejay and one of the hottest producers in the game, was onstage. The crowd was going crazy. The VIP section on the far side of the room housed all the ballers. Oh, snap! I knew that wasn't LeBron James in the house. The celebs were out and there was a sea of beautiful people on the dance floor.

I couldn't believe I was watching it all from the sidelines. I wasn't feelin' this grunt-work trick-bag crap Rico had put me in. I was breakin' my neck for this dude and he was throwing me crumbs. How could he do that to me? I needed to be hangin' with LeBron and his crew, not picking up their trash. I made up my mind. I was going to have to step to Rico about this, and I was going to figure out a way to get Tre and Mamie's CD played in this club.

CHAPTER TWENTY-TWO

COLLIN

I toss and turn, I keep stressing my mind.
—Kid Cudi, "Day and Night"

Whiteboy was being released today after four weeks in the hospital, and since Blue was nowhere around, I made sure I was there to pick him up. He was unusually quiet during my last visit. I could sense depression setting in. I knew it was going to be tough as he mentally prepared himself for the next level of therapy for his hand.

I pulled up to the hospital valet prepared to go in and help him check out, but he was already waiting for me in the doorway. I bet he gave those nurses hell getting out of there. His injured hand was wrapped and in a sling. He tossed his free arm in the air as if to shout *Freedom*. Whiteboy barely let me put the car in park before he had the door open. He immediately

hopped in and it was all over his face—he had no plans of coming back anytime soon.

"So how do you feel, man?" I asked, pulling off.

"Pissed that my face is still all jacked up with this wire for the next few weeks," he muttered. "I hate hospitals. They're worse than jail." We laughed.

We made it to Ms. H's house in no time. She was waiting out front.

"Tommy!" she shouted with elation; tears were running down her cheeks.

"Hi, Ms. H," I greeted, grabbing the plastic bag with Whiteboy's belongings from the backseat. She gave him a motherly hug and led us to the entrance to his apartment. I had never been inside his place before and was amazed by all the great art Whiteboy had done on the walls and ceilings of his basement studio apartment.

"Man, this stuff is incredible!" I said, setting his bag down and grabbing a seat in a nearby chair.

"I'm dope like that," he said with a pained expression, sitting down on the bed and leaning his back against the headboard. "So you and Blue talking yet?"

"Not really," I replied, sitting back in my chair.

"Man, I feel bad. I feel like drama always seems to follow me."

"Dude, I told you. We're so over the party. We may not be really speaking, but when we saw you in that hospital bed, it freaked us both out. Me and Blue and the whole Blue Up thing not working had *nothing* to do with you. He can never admit when he's wrong. It's time he knows. I'm fine with it all."

"I guess we can all be assholes sometimes, but in the end it's knowing who's down for you, right?" he said, wincing in pain. "Pass me that bottle of pain pills, yo." He pointed at the plastic bag.

"Actually, what's more important to me right now is working on having a better relationship with my father. I'm kickin' butt in school, preparing to go to Georgetown's summer program. I don't even want to cloud my mind with smoking weed or drinking. I haven't done either in weeks."

"Yeah, well, I would love anything to keep from facing the reality of a busted hand." He took the bottle of pills from me and opened it with his teeth. "On your pops, just remember why you got that tattoo that spells out 'Father.' You got it as a way of proclaiming your independence and manhood." Don't get so caught up in trying to be what he never was. You're a better dude, C. Stay true to yourself, feel me?"

"I feel you, man. But I'm doing this for me, for real. So, what about you? I know this is hard for you, Whiteboy. I'm just glad it wasn't worse and now you can move on, right?" He didn't respond. "Whiteboy?"

"I just know that now that I'm out, I've gotta handle my business," he said, staring at the ceiling.

"Yeah, I know you're gonna push yourself. Therapy will be over before you know it. You'll be back sketching and drawing in no time," I said.

"You can save all that optimistic bs. I mean *handle* my business with the fools that did this to me!" he said, sitting up.

"Dude, this time it was your jaw; next time it could be your life!"

"I can't believe I actually let some punks beat me down." He gave a menacing laugh. "C, I got a reputation!" A shot of pain made him take three quick breaths.

This was serious shit and I needed to talk some sense into Whiteboy. "I think it's been a long day and you need to get some rest. Tomorrow you'll wake up with a clear head."

"C, I've got a clear head." He paused. "I didn't tell you all, but I was accepted to the art institute here, full scholarship and everything." His voice had a hint of sarcasm.

"Dude, that's incredible! Why didn't you tell us?"

"I found out the day before the party. I was going to surprise you and Blue. I guess hearing you guys always talk about college motivated me. I don't know. But none of that matters anymore. My life isn't school, never has been. I was fooling myself to think that my life could be like y'all's. What all this did was help me realize that I gotta stay true to me and what I know."

"Whiteboy, you're trippin'! And those dudes don't have anything to live for. Screw that crap about revenge. How about this was a wake-up call for you to see that this is your opportunity to get out of that old life for good. Your art can take you all over the world. Dude, you don't ever have to see those dudes again."

"C, I may never draw again. Yo, where I'm from you can't let somebody do this to you and get away with it. Even though deep down I might not want to do this, I have to or I'll just be a mark at this point. Sometimes you have to do stuff like this even though you know you shouldn't. If I don't retaliate, everyone will see me as a punk and I'll never survive on these streets. Did you see me in that hospital? A fuckin' broken jaw! Whiteboy got beat down? Yo, they out here talkin' trash about me. Never again." He popped two Vicodins in his mouth, swallowed, and turned on his side with his back to me.

"Let it go, man. Just let it go," I said, turning to leave. "And by the way, you do have a future," I said, stopping. "You have real talent. You don't have to prove anything to anybody. The people that matter, me and Blue, know how real you are." He didn't respond.

About an hour or so later I joined my father for dinner.

"Do you know the difference between a Republican and a Democrat?" my father cracked. "Republicans just wear more expensive suits." There was an eruption of laughter that bellowed beneath a cloud of cigar smoke hovering above our table. Front row center, prime real estate on the prized mezzanine level of DC's hip hot spot and restaurant The Park at Fourteenth.

I was surrounded by a table of stiff suits with salt-and-pepper hair, sterling Tiffany cuff links, monogrammed custom-made dress shirts, and expensive watches—Breitling, Rolex, Cartier. These were my dad's "learned colleagues," "partners," or whatever you want to call them. They were lobbyists in the private sector, representing everything from trade associations to the pharmaceutical industry.

The good-old-boys club was celebrating the victory of my dad's partner Jay Taub, a robust, overly tanned Armani-clad dude. He was laughing the hardest and the loudest. My dad had invited me to sit ringside, to witness this sideshow of wealth and super-status success. Dad's firm had just landed a huge new client that represented the telecommunications industry.

I was going to be sick if I heard Harvard, Yale, University of Virginia, even Georgetown, one more time. I wanted to be any-place *but* here, and I wanted to be anything *but* my father. My entire life I'd dreamt of being a Georgetown Hoya. All I knew in life was the world of law. I was born into it. I inherited a thirst for it, like vampires do for blood. I knew I had what it took too. But I didn't want it like *this*. I was repulsed by what I saw and what my father's life was about.

I wanted to see the fruits of my labor make people enjoy life. Representing an artist who made music that made people fall in love or dance or kick it with their boys was so far removed from what these guys did. My dad and his comrades made sure the rich got richer. Screw the poor or the people working hard to have decent healthcare. That just wasn't me.

My father and I returned home from our barbaric feast. He downed two more Jack and Cokes, patted himself on the back a few more times, and reminded me that one day *this* would all be mine, before finally disappearing into his bedroom. I quietly slipped out the side door and dashed through the yard to the pool house.

I knocked lightly on the door twice but didn't get an answer. The door was slightly ajar. I pushed it slowly and knocked lightly again.

"Mamie, it's me, Collin," I whispered.

"Fool, you scared me!" Mamie loudly whispered, holding her chest as if I had startled her.

"I'm sorry. I just need to talk."

"C'mon in before your dad hears us."

I entered and plopped down on the chaise longue next to the bed. She removed her headphones.

"Whassup, C?" she asked. Wrinkles formed across her forehead.

I leaned my head back and rested it in the cradle of my clasped hands, letting out a sigh. "I just came from an enlightening dinner meeting with my dad."

"Sounds amazing to me. I don't get the worried look on your face."

"It was enlightening because it opened my eyes and showed me where I *didn't* want my life to end up. I just keep thinking about my brother, Kyle, and how his death ripped my mother to the core, and my dad is still keeping all that pain inside. Guilt can eat away at you if you let it.

"Then I take Whiteboy home from the hospital and he's so angry he wants to go after the guys who did this to him. It's a vicious cycle. He's not even realizing that we're his family and what it would do to us if he gets killed or goes to jail for good. I used to think about taking myself out a lot after my brother's overdose, but I knew it would destroy my mother." I rubbed my hands through my hair. "I have regrets about what happened between me and Blue. I don't know if we can ever even be civil again. But I wonder how it all got like this." I let out a labored sigh. "I'm rambling and you probably think I'm crazy, huh? I'm on some distant planet and everyone else is in another solar system."

"C, stop, you're not crazy. You're taking on too much," she said, scooting to the edge of the bed and touching my hand. "I normally just try to listen, because who am I to be judgmental or criticize or, hell, even offer advice? Look at my life. But as your friend, your homegirl, someone who loves you dearly, I gotta say my peace. I mean, you're probably the only guy who I've ever trusted enough to talk to about my family, my dreams, my life, who never wanted anything from me. Not my beats, not sex, not anything but my friendship." She leaned in closer.

"C, it's time that you be okay with who Collin is, feel me? Stop taking on everybody else's pain."

"What do you mean?"

"I mean, you're Collin, you're *not* your dad, and you're not Kyle, or your mom, or Blue, or Whiteboy, or me. You can't fix everything. At the end of the day you have to live your life. And not that my opinion means anything, but you and Blue are probably the only ones who can get through to Whiteboy. Me? My parents aren't around, school didn't work for me, and I don't even have my aunt in my corner anymore. My life is completely screwed, but the one thing I have going for me is my dream and I ain't giving up on it! I have to look to the future. I can't look back."

Her words struck me to the core so deeply, there were no words to respond with. Mamie and I embraced for a long time and it felt good. I kissed her on her forehead and said good night. For the next hour or so I lay awake in bed, staring at the ceiling. They say that everything in the dark eventually comes to light. It was time that my mom, dad, and even I stopped holding on to the past and living in the dark. The first step is being truthful and sometimes the truth hurts.

I tried to close my eyes, but they popped back open. I kept thinking about Whiteboy trying to go after those guys. I hoped he wouldn't do anything stupid. The thought of what Mamie said about Blue and me being the only ones Whiteboy would listen to was weighing me down like a ton of bricks. As much as my better judgment would argue against it, I whipped out my cell and shot off a text to Blue.

NEED 2 TALK . . . C

A few minutes later my phone buzzed:

BEEN THINKIN' THE SAME THING MEET ME @
THE BLEACHERS @ LUNCH 2MORROW

COOL

CHAPTER TWENTY-THREE

BLUE

Even grass grow baby
You know seeds become plants, boys become men
—Usher featuring Jay-Z, "Best Thing"

When I saw my boy Collin walking toward the football field bleachers, it actually felt bittersweet, like long-lost brothers who had been fighting reuniting. I waved him over to where I was sitting.

"What's good?" I greeted. The mood was definitely uncomfortable. So much so that we didn't even give each other a pound, fist-tap, nothing. We sat down. "Thanks for hittin' me up. But what brought that on?"

"I guess everything between us has been bothering me for a while. But I felt I had a point to prove."

"Yeah, me too." I nodded.

"But it all really hit home after I picked up Whiteboy

from the hospital. He wants revenge on those guys who jumped him."

"He could get killed for real this time."

"Or kill somebody else. I think we've got to find a way to get through to him." He paused, shaking his head. "And the part that really got me was that he told me he'd gotten accepted to art school. Apparently he found out the day before the party. He was going to surprise us."

"We can't let any of this go down," I said, shaking my head.

"I know. I mean, it really hit me how fleeting life can be. He doesn't see it that way, but maybe together we could help him see how stupid the whole idea of retaliation is."

"I'm with you. So what next?"

"Well, he's just as stubborn as we are, except what he feels he has to prove is on a whole other level. We gotta talk him out of it. Simple as that!"

"Damn, it took all of this to get us to come back to our senses, huh? I can't believe I was on a mission to prove to you and everybody else that I still had it. That I could make Blue Up happen regardless of what anybody else had to say. Things jumped off at first, and I admit I let it go to my head. My ego was out of control."

"What?" Collin went wide-eyed. "Okay, maybe I should get that in writing." We both started laughing.

"Yeah, except somewhere along the way it started to come apart. We fell out, Jade broke things off, her mom being so sick, and my dad and I aren't getting along," I said, as the period bell rang in the distance. I stood up, grabbed my backpack, and tossed it over my shoulder. Collin did the same.

"I'm sorry that I had to bail on you with Blue Up, but it got too intense for me."

"It's cool, C. I know the potential Blue Up has, but I've gotta crawl before I can walk, right?"

"More like run before you fly when it comes to you!"

"Yeah, yeah, my point is, I can handle you having to step away. I even dealt with the Rico Tate situation."

"Word?" Collin said with surprise as we walked down the steps onto the track field.

"Yep, you're officially looking at his new protégé!" We gave each other a high five. "I made a deal to basically work off the money owed. C, we made ten Gs that night and he kept all that dough. On top of that he added another five Gs."

"Yikes! That's gangsta, man!"

"I know, but sometimes you have to pay for your mistakes in sweat. So, I can do that. I realize now that you didn't leave me out there hangin'. Honestly, I probably left you out there. Sometimes I move before I think. I'm working on that. I'm working on not being so selfish, too."

"I'm impressed, Blue, but same goes for me. I've been a real asshole."

"Let's just squash all the beefin'," I said, offering an olive branch by holding out a solid fist. He returned the gesture and we tapped fists.

"I guess I get my stubbornness from my father. Isn't that ironic?"

"That's crazy, man, my dad has been all over me about getting my act together in school. But it wasn't until Rico made it clear school had to come first did I focus on the books."

"That's because the entertainment game drives you. Your dad may never get it. I know my dad won't. But join the club: He's been making me check in like I'm in the military." We shared a laugh. "I've made up my mind that I'm going to fulfill my father's wishes and see this Georgetown summer program through."

"Then he should be proud, C."

"That's to be determined, but I'm cool. I do what I have to do so I can get where I need to go in life."

"I like that!" I said, stopping and patting him on the shoulder. "Brothers to the end, right?"

"Till the bitter end, dude!" We gave each other a rowdy pound. "Man, I think we're all going through some bad times right now. Mamie's aunt kicked her out, and then she dropped out of school. She's been crashing at my place."

"Yo, and you haven't tried to push up on that?"

"C'mon, dude. I keep telling you she's my *friend*. That's it. Mamie's sexy and all, but we're not into each other on that level."

"I'm impressed, C. Well, looks like Jade has a college guy. Do me a favor and get the scoop."

"Yeah right, Mamie never drops dime on Jade."

"Work your magic. I've got faith, bro! Look, I'm workin' the club tonight so I'd better hit the library." We gave each other a high five and headed back into SSH.

Despite all the bad things that had happened, our friendship had become stronger than before. Although, it felt like we were at some crazy crossroads. But what that crossroads was exactly, I couldn't figure out. I just hoped we could talk some sense into Whiteboy.

CHAPTER TWENTY-FOUR

WHITEBOY

I know the storm is comin
My pockets keep tellin' me it's gonna shower
—Flo Rida, "Right Round"

Ms. H smiled, handing me a glass of carrot juice and an unopened envelope with a return address that read: *Peter Mason, Associate Professor, Art Institute of Washington*. I opened it and scanned through the letter. It was my official letter of acceptance into the school, and my scholarship award.

"Tommy, God make no mistake. You gotta chance, *mijo*," She winked, touching my face before returning upstairs.

I sat down at my art table and placed the letter in front of me. I was still having a lot of pain from the couple of broken ribs, which were taped up. I popped a pain pill in my mouth and flipped open my sketch pad. I placed my right hand on the blank page, picked up a pair of scissors, and slowly began to cut open the soft cast. I removed it and began to unwrap the bandages, peeling them away, layer after layer.

I swallowed hard and closed my eyes as I pulled away the final bandage. I hadn't seen my hand since the night of the fight. I had to be ready mentally to look at it. I reopened my eyes and grimaced at the sight of all the stitches from two surgeries. Holding my hand in the air, I examined it closer. It looked skinny and weak. My fingers were stiff and it was hard to move them. I could barely make a fist. I put my hand back down on the blank page of the sketch pad. It was as empty as my thoughts.

I picked up my pencil with my left hand and with several light strokes began to sketch. I didn't know where I was going with it. I just needed to release some of this pinned-up energy. But I wasn't a lefty. The drawing was horrible. I ripped up the page and slammed my pencil down. I felt my chest tighten with anger.

I grabbed my cell phone and typed a quick text to my man Wiz.

YO ITS WHITEBOY HOW U?

WORD? U ALIVE?

IN THE FLESH BABY!

I HEARD ABOUT WHAT WENT DOWN

I'M A SOLDIER! SO WHASSUP U SEEN THAT FOOL LOPEZ

NOBODY HAS, BUT YA BOY ROOK IS BACK

I NEED TO HOLLA @ U

U KNOW WHERE TO FIND ME HOLLA

LATER

I had a mission on my mind and that was final.

Just then I heard a knock on my door, followed by a familiar voice. "Yo, knock, knock, is Picasso up in this beeyach!" It was Blue outside my door.

"One minute!" I shouted back, quickly rewrapping my hand and putting my arm back in the sling. When I opened the door Blue and Collin were standing there with big corny grins on their faces.

"We're here to award you with the Art Institute of Washington's one-hundred-thousand-dollar presidential scholarship!"

"Aw, so y'all got jokes!" They laughed, pushing their way inside. Blue made himself comfortable on a nearby chair, and Collin grabbed a chair, turned it backward, and sat down.

"Dude, we just wanted to welcome you home in style," Collin said.

"So, y'all back!" I said.

"Wonder Twins activated, baby!" Blue shouted.

"The Dynamic Duo, in effect!" Collin added.

"Man, I'm just happy to see that you guys patched things up. That was killing me," I said.

"Yeah, we realized we had both been wrong," Collin said, looking at Blue.

"Definitely," he added.

"So how's the club goin', Blue?" I asked.

"Oh, you remember? You know you dissed me hard that day at the hospital. But I deserved it. The club is hard work, but the even better news is that Mamie and Tre did a mix CD and the first copies sold like crazy. Fools was feelin' the CD artwork especially," Blue said.

"Word?" I smiled as best I could through the wires. "That's hot, that's real hot!"

"So, you look good, man," Collin said.

"Yeah, well, y'all gotta see me like this. Just ready to get back to work," I said, looking down at my hand. "But I don't think that's gonna ever happen."

"In due time. But, um, don't you mean get school jumpin' off?" Blue asked.

"Aw, C, you told?" Whiteboy said, shaking his head.

"It's great news!" Collin replied.

"We're proud of you, man," Blue said. "What's going on with registering for art school?" He held his hand up in a what's-up-with-that gesture.

"Yo, that ain't me no more," I said. I was distracted when my phone vibrated. I checked the screen.

I THINK I KNOW WHERE U CAN FIND ROOK DEF
GET AT ME 2DAY—PEACE, WIZ

I quickly closed the screen. "What I do know is that I got an appointment. It's all good, and I'm cool on all that art school stuff right now," I said, quickly brushing Blue and Collin off. "I won't be takin' them up on their offer." I shook my head. "Look at me. Plus, I've got some other more pressing things going on." Collin and Blue looked at each other, then eyed me suspiciously.

"I hope it's not what we think it is," Blue said, resting his elbows on his knees and leaning forward with a tightened expression. I cut my eyes at Collin.

"I'm sorry, but yeah, I told Blue. As your friends, we weren't going to sit by and not say or do anything!" Collin stressed.

"As your real friends!" Blue said. "Don't try to go after that guy Lopez. Let it go, man! You got a chance. But you won't get that again if you try to retaliate against those fools."

"I look like a punk to you or somethin'!" I felt myself getting charged up. I flinched from a sharp pain in my rib cage. I grabbed my abdomen with my left hand and took a deep breath.

"Look, you might be cool with gettin' taken out for real this time or going to jail for life, but we're your boys. That ain't cool with us!" Collin stressed.

"Whiteboy, let them haters die like dogs!" Blue said.

"Y'all done? 'Cause I got things to do. I need to get to therapy," I said with a stony expression.

"It's cool, we'll leave you alone," Blue said.

"Hey, we love you, man. We don't want to see you go down. Lopez is gonna get his one way or the other, and it won't be because of your hands. You don't live that life anymore. You got opportunity," Collin said as they both got up.

We gave each other a round of pounds. My homies knew when to drop a subject. I had business to take care of. What I didn't want to do was involve them in any of that. My priority right now was getting to Rook to find out why he set me up, and taking down Lopez. I put on my sweats and sneaks and was out.

I pulled up in front of the pool hall and spotted Wiz. Wiz was one of those cats whose eyes and ears were everywhere. I needed to get with Rook to find out what the real deal with him and Lopez was, and confront him about why I took the fall for his dirt. He owed me.

"Whassup, Wiz." I nodded.

"Oh, yo! Whassup, young? You really are alive! I'm real happy to see you. Word got out that maybe you was dead or something. That clown Lopez been poppin' off at the mouth that you got *got*!"

"Nah, young, never that. You see me, don't you? He got me, you see that, but he had to have his crew with him. I don't need no crew. I took some heat for some beef that ain't mine, and he caught me slippin'. You know, I'm tryin' to live right. But it's cool. You know I'm not goin' out like that. You seen Rook?" I asked, tightening my expression.

"I heard he burned out, young. Maybe went up to Philly or down to Atlanta."

"So what were you sayin' about knowing where Rook was?"

"Supposedly Rook is back in the studio nightly," he said, leaning in close to me. "So, whassup?"

"Look, I might be needing something," I said, squinting.

Before I could blink, Wiz was popping the trunk to his truck, which was parked in the alley behind Joe's.

"What's your flavor?" he asked, eyeing me, showing off a display of handguns. "All the serial numbers have been removed too."

I looked down at his small arsenal, then back at him. I stared at him long and hard. I had a choice to make. The stakes were high this time, higher than ever.

CHAPTER TWENTY-FIVE

BLUE

I party like a rock star
Look like a movie star
—Pitbull, "Go Girl"

"Señor Reynolds? Señor Reynolds? *¡Vamanos!*" my Spanish teacher, Ms. Rodriguez, shouted and clapped her hands loudly, startling me. I was the last one sitting at my desk in the classroom. Class was over and I apparently had fallen asleep. *¿Qué es tu problema?*"

"Huh?"

"Mr. Reynolds, you slept through half my class!" she snapped. "Perhaps you should modify your social life if you're not getting enough sleep at home." She handed me my Spanish test on my way out. My face lit up.

"B plus! Sweet! Second time in a row!" I shouted. I'd never made anything higher than a C in Spanish before this term.

It was the one class I'd always dreaded. Off her expression, I quickly exited.

I was beat down, but I had to keep telling myself it was all going to be worth it. Otherwise, I didn't know how long I could keep pulling crazy weekend hours and busting my butt during the week. Big Mike told me to be at the club thirty minutes later tonight. I used to get hyped on TGIF; I wasn't so sure anymore. But I guessed I had to just keep thinking about guys like Diddy. I was sure he had a lot of sleepless days and weeks. I had to stay motivated and keep in mind that the payoff was going to be phenomenal!

As soon as the parentals were asleep, I got dressed for the club. I had their routine down to the minute, and sneaking out was getting almost too easy. I did my usual move and slipped out my window, smoothly hopped in the car, and was out. I was getting used to my getaway route out of the house, and everyone at the club knew my name and I knew theirs.

Before I got out of the car I picked up Mamie and Tre's mix. I was holding gold in my hands. I decided tonight I was going to make my move with it. If Rico wasn't feelin' it, then I was determined to get *somebody* to listen.

By twelve o'clock the club was packed. I was envious of Rico. Man, if this was my joint, I'd be making crazy money. I watched Rico work the room from afar. He greeted every party-goer in sight, especially the ladies, making sure everyone was having a good time. Rico especially rolled out the red carpet for the ballers, giving that VIP his or her own personal valet and hostess. I watched how meticulous Rico was about who was allowed to step behind the velvet rope into the VIP area. You had to be somebody of ballerific proportions or super-model status.

The deejay mixed in another hot one. I was engrossed in watching Rico's flow, his style, his swagger. He was better than any politician I'd ever seen. Rico shook hands, kissed attractive women's cheeks, gave pounds to NBA and NFL players, and in the midst of all his smoothness, staff ran up to him periodically, whispering updates on the club happenings. He had eyes everywhere.

When I saw that he had a few minutes to himself, I made my move.

"Rico, I just wanted to say thank you again for giving me a shot to fix the money situation. Seeing you in action opened my eyes, and now I understand this game on a whole new level."

"Even if it's to take out some trash or mop the floors?" he said with a sly grin.

"Hey, I gotta do what I gotta do."

"Yeah, like your hustle, Blue. You stick with me and I'm gonna make you a star!"

"Um, Rico, by the way, here's a copy of the new and improved Young Tre. It's his mix, featuring *and* produced by Ill Mama."

"I ain't got time to listen to that right now, but follow me. I need you to handle something." I was ready to blow! What did he need me to do next? Probably clean up an overflowing toilet. Dejected, I put the CD back in my pocket

"I want you to meet someone," Rico said, as I followed closely behind. He led me up the stairs to the level where the music was all hip-hop.

When we got to a roped-off area that was furnished with low plush ottomans, I noticed a guy in large dark shades, dressed head to toe in what I was sure was some expensive Italian designer gear, topped off with a pair of fresh, crispy white sneaks. He was cool-looking in an eclectic kind of way. Rico and the guy greeted each other like old buddies.

"JD Stone, my man!" Rico gave the man a pound after they hugged. "This is my young protégé, Blue Reynolds," Rico shouted over the music. I couldn't believe he was actually introducing me like that. I shook JD's hand enthusiastically. "I just wanted to make sure you were having a good time, and if you need anything, Blue can get it."

"This club is always one of the hottest spots on the East Coast. You know every now and then I have to give New York a break and come back and visit my hometown. It's crazy tonight, thanks for inviting me up. The music is great!" JD said.

"Make sure you take care of my boy," Rico whispered in my ear.

"You sure?" I whispered back.

"I'm always sure!" he said, patting me on the back. Just then his assistant called him over to handle an urgent matter. While JD got back to the bevy of babes that surrounded him, I stood out like a cornball. At least three songs had passed and it was like I wasn't even there.

"Excuse me, Mr. Stone, can I get you anything?" I asked loudly, tapping JD on his shoulder.

"I'm busy right now, kid," he said, offering a not so polite smile. JD Stone wasn't as cool as I thought.

"No problem, Rico just wanted me to look out for you. Would you like anything to eat or drink? I can get a waiter over."

"I'm not hungry and I don't drink. Look, just make yourself busy and grab me a bottle of Voss water."

I dashed off to get JD's water and made it back with stunning alacrity. I was not about to keep Mr. A-hole waiting.

"What's it like producing the show?" one of the women fawning over him said. My ears perked up.

"Basically, I'm responsible for taking talent to the next level. Every rap kid in America wants to be discovered, and that's just what they get on *106 and Park*," he bragged.

I swear I wasn't trying to stare, but the wheels in my mind were churning as I watched JD's every move. He was just the guy to get Tre's mix to. If Tre could get on *106 & Park* and win Freestyle Friday, he'd be on his way.

"Yo, kid, you makin' me mad nervous. Why are you staring at me?" JD interrupted my thoughts.

"I'm sorry, Mr. Stone, but I overheard what you and, um," I choked.

"Time is money, kid!"

"Um, see, I'm working with this cat who's a beast on the mic. His name is Young Tre. He's my artist. I just wanted to slip you my artist's mix CD. He really needs to be on Freestyle Friday. He could kill the champion."

"Is that right?" he replied, but I wasn't about to back down. "So let's see how fire this Young Tre really is," he said with a sly grin.

"Absolutely. Hold on!" At that point I don't know what came over me, but I knew I had to take my chance. I raced over, tapped on the deejay booth window, and waved Tre's CD to the deejay.

"Hey, this is some new fire. Rico wants to get it on right away," I said. I was lying, and Rico was probably going to kill me, but I may not ever again get this close to getting Young Tre on *106 & Park*.

"This is messing up my whole flow," the deejay said, giving me an incredulous look.

"Yo, you've gotta get it on right away, or that's my ass! And Jay-Z's even backing it!" I emphatically replied, looking over at a chuckling JD. I swallowed hard, praying to God the crowd wouldn't think it was wack. The deejay was pissed, but I didn't care at that point.

Seconds later when the track came on, it was like the whole room stopped. I could tell they were trying to figure out what that song was. An intense go-go beat breakdown kicked the track off, followed by a baseline that made the whole building shake. All of a sudden the room went crazy, and the party was kicked into overdrive. Everyone rushed to the dance floor. I made my way back over to him.

"Yo, who is this kid on the track again?" JD smiled, bobbing his head.

"His name is Young Tre. He's from right here. Anacostia!" I quickly shouted over the music.

"I dig him. We may be able to give him a shot!" He winked.

Just as JD Stone gave me a thumbs-up, Rico re-entered the VIP area.

"Yo, I like this kid's hustle!" JD winked. Rico quickly figured out that I had orchestrated the entire shift of the party and made his prize VIP *very* happy. He gave me a look of approval.

I wasted no time giving JD my cell number, and he rattled off his. I had played my move smoothly and even left the great Rico Tate in a state of shock.

CHAPTER TWENTY-SIX

JADE

**Baby I can see your halo
You know you're my saving grace
—Beyoncé, "Halo"**

I would've never imagined this day, this moment. The sting-ing pools of tears that had formed in my eyes just sat there. I couldn't blink, I couldn't breathe. I was the weak one and my mother was the one so strong, sitting up, frail, gaunt, and smiling like things were okay, but they weren't. They were far from okay.

"I have six months, Jade." I tried to blink again, but my eye-lids were stuck. I needed someone to pinch me. None of this was real, right? "Jade, say something, baby." She sat reaching out to me. At that instant I turned into a mound of Jell-O. The most horrific cry fought like hell to get out. I opened my mouth, but nothing came out. My mother had six months to live and that just wasn't fair. I felt my body slowly breaking into a million pieces. I gently fell into her frail arms. And then the tears poured and they kept coming. I was light-headed and confused. How could this be? She was supposed to be getting better.

"Baby, listen to me. I'm so proud of you and you've been my rock through all this."

"But, Mama, you have to see me graduate. You have to see me become a doctor. You have to see me walk down the aisle and have children," I wailed. I just wanted time to stop and rewind.

"Why? Why can't these damn doctors fix things!" I shouted.

"Get it all out. It's okay, Jade," she said, pulling me close. "I know this is so tough." She pulled back and put her hand on my face. "Listen to me, sweetface. There comes a time in life when we have to grow up, even parents. I'm going to fight like hell, because that's what we do. But I want us to live like we've never lived before. Do you hear me, Jade?" she demanded, looking me in the eyes. "I want us to talk about everything and I promise there's no question that I won't answer."

I tried to think of questions, but I didn't know where to begin. I was numb. Suddenly, the only thing that had become more important than wondering about her death was knowing about her life. My mother was being taken away from me, and when she was gone I'd have nothing. No connections to grandparents, a few distant cousins, no siblings, and most important, no knowledge of where or who my father was. She never talked about him. I'd lived almost eighteen years with this question mark hanging over me.

"Who's my father?"

"What?" She was confused and thrown off by my question.

"You said you'd answer anything, well, that's what I want to know now that you're dying." My voice quivered.

"Jade, I don't think that's something we should talk about right now."

"When, then? When you go I'll have no one. What about *me*!"

"Jade, you have a right to be angry, but know that I've loved you the only way I know how."

"By lying to me. It's not fair that this is happening and I have no one to lean on. God is going to take you away. What did I ever do to anyone that would make me deserve this! Huh?" Tears were streaming down my face. I grabbed my purse and stormed out.

CHAPTER TWENTY-SEVEN

BLUE

Chillin' with a boss . . . you like the way I floss
—Trey Songz, "Famous"

I stopped by the club before heading home by special request from Rico.

"Blue," he said, sitting on the edge of his desk. "Our debt is settled."

"Really?" I said with surprise. "So, I'm done here?" I was confused.

"Not quite. You've shown me that you aren't afraid to hustle. You definitely impressed JD Stone."

"Look, Rico, I'm sorry about that. I just saw an opportunity and I knew I had to seize it."

"You definitely did that." He smirked. "You even had DJ Future shook. Good line, I actually like how you tossed the boss's name at him."

"I didn't mean any harm."

"Let me tell you a secret: As long as you aren't committing murder, taking food out of a baby's mouth, or disrespecting your parents, and there are few more in between those, it's fair game."

"Um, wow, okay," I said, getting up from my chair.

"Even though your debt is paid, I think I want to keep you around." My heart started beating fast. "I like the whole protégé thing." He extended his hand. "I'm thinkin' of revisiting the whole teen night idea, but we gotta work some kinks out. When we do, I want Young Tre and Ill Mama to headline. What do you think?"

"I think, wow!"

"We'll work out the details later." I shook Rico's hand vigorously. I had passed the test like the last Samurai and was ready for the next level. If I lock in *106 & Park*, there would be no turning back!

Things were moving in all the right directions, but I had another debt to settle up. None of this would've been possible without Chuck.

I caught the rec center door just as it was closing. Chuck was standing talking with a small group of staffers on the other side of the room. The place was buzzing with workers setting up for what looked like a massive party. Chuck was just finishing a meeting. I stood off to the side, still out of breath from running all the way to the center from the Metro station three blocks away.

"Thanks a lot, team. Let's change a young person's life today!" Chuck rallied the troops for a group high five. When he saw my face, his expression hardened. As everyone dispersed, I called out to him.

"Hey, Chuck, can I talk to you for a minute?" I rushed up to him. He folded his arms across his chest, an immediate signal that he didn't want to hear what I had to say. "I'm really sorry I haven't been around like I promised."

"Blue, been around? C'mon, young bro, you disappeared." He chuckled. "But I'll give it to you, you played it, as the kids say, real *gangsta*. You basically used me. If all you wanted was a hook up, you should've said that from the beginning. Now, if you'll excuse me. Our opening gala is tomorrow." He started to walk away.

"Wait, Chuck, please hear me out. I'm sorry—" My words were halted by an exhausted look, beyond disgust. "I got caught up in trying to not just be in the mix but *be* the mix.

"Blue, you're still a kid, and like I told you before, you got a lot of lessons to learn. I don't fault you. I fault my own judgment. There was a time I wouldn't let people off the hook so easily, but I guess I saw real potential in you. Unfortunately, you've been a disappointment."

"Chuck, please don't give up on me," I pleaded. "Look," I said, pulling out Tre and Mamie's CD and handing it to him. He reluctantly took it. "Look, I'm living up to part of my word. I'm committed to my artists. I hustled at Rico's club to pay him back, and I even brought all my grades up. I'm serious about school!"

"Do you see all this?" He pointed around the room. "Do you see all the preparations being made for the gala? This is my destiny. You can hustle around and give everybody lip service and try to be a jack-of-all-trades, but you still end up with crumbs. It's about backing up all the talk. You didn't honor your word," he said, holding his arms out and shrugging his shoulders. "Stop with the excuses. I haven't heard from you. You made a deal with me. I'd help you out with some valuable advice in exchange for some of your valuable time."

"But see, Chuck, it's been tough getting things on track."

"Young bro, you still don't get it." He shook his head. "I hope one day you do for *your* sake. See, I've made my millions, Blue. But these kids need their shot," he said, pointing to the kids playing on the outdoor basketball court, then toward the glass-enclosed tutor rooms filled with kids and volunteers.

"I wanted to see you get your shot. But sometimes we have to step outside our own world and give back just a little. You blew it! I've gotta go. I've given you enough of my time. Just remember there's a difference between good and great, and dreamers who never live up to their potential and dream-makers who call the shots. I got no time for empty promises. The center will be here when you get your mind right. I'm not going to chase you down." Chuck winked. He had made his point loud and clear.

His words reverberated in my head as I walked out of the center. Chuck was my biggest fan, but he just straight shut me down. I did try to do the right thing. I guess I was too late. I was kicking myself big-time as I walked toward the Metro.

Just then the sound of a horn honking came from behind me.

"Blue! Blue!" I turned around just as Chuck was pulling up next to me. "I'm going against my better judgment again, but if I give up on you, that would be like giving up on one of my kids at the center." I felt a smile creep across my face. "So I'm gonna give you one last chance."

"Bet, I won't let you down," I eagerly replied.

"That mix CD is incredible. Have the girl deejay and the rapper kid here tomorrow. I want them to perform at the gala!" I walked up to the driver's window and gave him a pound.

"They'll be here, and I'd like another shot at volunteering here too."

"How about we get through tomorrow and then we'll talk, because once you give me your word, you can't turn back. Hop in—I'll drop you at the Metro."

I jumped in the passenger seat and we zoomed off. All

I could do was breathe a sigh of relief. Chuck had saved my butt again. I had to make good on my word this time for sure. I quickly typed out a text to Mamie and Tre:

I JUST BOOKED U GUYS A SHOW @ THE REC CENTER GALA 2MORROW IT'S ON!!!

CHAPTER TWENTY-EIGHT

MAMIE

You can say good-bye, you can say hello
But you'll always find your way back home
—Miley Cyrus, "You'll Always Find Your Way Back Home"

Blue's message last night made my entire year, and Tre invited me over for dinner to celebrate and run through the order of the show. No guy had ever invited me over for dinner with his family. Kind of weird, but cool at the same time. Since it was his grandparents and all, I figured I'd better try to look conservative. I thought they went to church a lot, too. I couldn't tell you when the last time I went to church was.

I definitely believed in God, but I'd never really been around anyone who went to church regularly. I figured a simple black dress and my pointy-toe flats were safest. I definitely didn't want to rock the stilettos in front of grandma!

I couldn't believe I was actually nervous when Tre opened the door.

"Whassup? You look good." He smiled.

"Hey, thanks. So do you," I nervously replied. Miles of course was being his regular smooth self, pushing past Tre and trying to hug a sista extra long. "Whassup, Miles a Million!"

"It's all on you," he said. I could feel his eyes following my butt as Tre led me into the dining room. I stopped and whispered in Tre's ear. "So how hyped are you about the show tonight?" I gave him a high five.

"We don't have any real rehearsal time, so let's just roll with something like we did at Club Heat that night."

"Whatever y'all do is gonna kill it!" Miles added.

Tre's grandmother interrupted us when she announced that dinner was ready. I was glad. I hadn't had a decent home-cooked meal since my aunt kicked me out.

"The Lord, smile upon us, make us thankful for this meal we are about to receive. Let it nourish our minds and bodies. And let your angels, my dear sweet Michelle and her dedicated and loving husband, Antonio, rest in peace." Sweets got choked up when she said the blessing.

"Sorry, she always gets a little emotional about my mother and father," Tre whispered to me.

"So, Mamie, Tre says you make music," his grandmother Sweets said, passing the mashed potatoes.

"Yes, ma'am, I'm a deejay and I make music from samples in old records, and also with the computer."

"Humph, well I guess I'll see tonight at the rec center's party?" Sweets chuckled.

"Well, ma'am, I really think you're gonna enjoy it."

"Still doesn't sound like music to me." Sweets fussed as she bit into a forkful of green beans.

"Sweets, it's how kids make music today," Miles added with a laugh.

"I knew that. Even I watch the hip-hop videos on BET," Pop Pop added. The table broke into laughter.

"Ma'am, I'm actually thinking about learning how to play the piano, though," Mamie said.

"I don't know about this hip-hop mess, but Tre plays the piano beautifully!" Sweets bragged. I could see she was embarrassing him.

After dinner and a few more laughs, Tre gave us a treat and played practically an entire concert for us on the piano. I had never heard someone play the way he played. Then, when he was done, he picked up his guitar and serenaded his grandparents. How sweet! We gave him a standing ovation when he finished. I felt like they were the family I'd been missing my whole life.

I checked the time and saw it was getting late. I had a few things to do before the show. Tre walked me out.

"Why didn't you ever tell me you played not *just* the piano but the guitar too? Boy, you don't need my tracks, you can make your own."

"Nah, you got something special. Maybe we can do a music collabo some time, though," I said.

"I'd like that." There was a nice moment of silence and I noticed just how cute Tre really was. "So, um, anyway, we should go over the show rundown. I need to go get ready and then I guess we can meet there."

"Sounds good!"

We sat outside on the front steps, and as I beat boxed, he spit his verses. Just like that we had our show together. That's when you know it's right! I checked my watch and gave him a good-bye hug. I couldn't wait to get on that stage with him. We were gonna rock the house tonight!

CHAPTER TWENTY-NINE

BLUE

'Cause I wanna be on *106 and Park* pushing a Benz
I wanna act ballerific like it's all terrific
—Kanye West, "All Falls Down"

**WANT TO GIVE YOUNG TRE A SHOT ON 106 & PARK . . .
STAY TUNED PEACE—JD STONE**

The Chuck Davis Recreational Complex was on and poppin' and the spot to be in tonight. The mayor, local dignitaries, community leaders, even some of the players on the Redskins were there. This was the place to be, and Tre and Mamie would be taking the stage soon. Me and Collin were in a private waiting area at the back of the center, waiting for Mamie and Tre to arrive. I bit my bottom lip and tapped my foot.

"Blue, why do you look so pensive?" Collin asked, tapping me on the shoulder. "Tonight is supposed to be a happy occasion.

You remember, Young Tre, Ill Mama, the dopest duo in hip-hop since Wyclef Jean and Lauryn Hill."

"I think I'm just nervous, but check this out." I whipped out my Sidekick and flashed him the message from JD Stone.

"That's incredible!" We did a fist-tap.

"I'm really glad you came, C."

Just then the stars of the hour entered. Tre was giving that Andre 3000 vibe, and Mamie was rockin' a plaid schoolgirl skirt, white blouse, and red stilettos, but Miles was probably looking like the biggest star wearing aviator glasses, fresh Chucks, jeans, a blazer, and a white tee.

"I see y'all came to win tonight!" I said as Collin gave dap to Tre and a hug to Mamie. "Lookin' fly, Miles!" I greeted, giving him a pound. "Yo, this is my boy Collin. C, this is Miles, Tre's cousin."

"Just call me Killa Cali!" Miles beamed, giving Collin a pound.

"Look, I want y'all to blow that stage up," I said, giving a last-minute pep talk. "Also, I wanted to wait until we got a confirmation, but seems like now is a good time. I can't promise anything, but I may have gotten you guys a strong shot on *106 and Park*!" The room exploded in high fives and pounds.

When the cheering died down, I tapped Collin. "Yo, C, let me holla at you," I said, motioning for him to follow me into the hallway.

"What's up?" he said.

"Look, I don't want to panic or anything, but when you mentioned Whiteboy a few minutes ago, it hit me that he was actin' real funny when I last spoke to him. He's been that way since he got out of the hospital."

"Man, I thought it was just me," Collin said. "I'm a little worried because I haven't been able to reach him all day, and that just doesn't seem right. The doctor took the wires off his jaw, but he's still supposed to be taking it easy."

"Why don't we just roll by there after the show?" I suggested.

"I'm with it, but you know how he gets. Let's play it cool. We just need to be supportive and not seem like we're trying to lecture him."

"Cool." We headed back into the room, and although I was in sync with everything Collin was saying, I still couldn't let go of the uneasy feeling I had.

Just then, Chuck popped his head into the room. "Five minutes, guys!" he called out.

"Chuck! My dude!" I shouted, giving him a pound. "Thanks for the opportunity. You remember Collin, of course, Young Tre, and Mamie, and this is Miles, Young Tre's cousin." Handshakes, hellos, and more thank-yous floated around the group. "By the way, Miles is nasty with a football in case you get any athletic programs going on."

"I do a li'l somethin' somethin'!" Miles flashed a modest yet confident smile.

"Well, check this out, young bro, as soon as we get our football league going, I want you to come try out!" Chuck gave Miles a pound as we made our way out to the stage in the center's auditorium. "Hey, Blue, I'm glad your dad could make it," Chuck said, leading the way.

"Huh?" I yelped, continuing to follow him. I punched Collin inconspicuously in the arm. My eyes went wide.

"Oh, crap! Dude, you are so busted."

Busted wasn't even the half of it. Me, Collin, and Miles stood on the side of the stage while Tre and Mamie rocked the house. They had old and young throwing their hands in the air. Meanwhile, I was sweating profusely as I watched my dad in the front row next to Tre's grandparents, stone-faced. Nobody could deny how insane the show was, even Sweets was clapping and dancing to the beat. Not Pops. This was going to be brutal.

"I'm Young Tre, and you're rockin' to the flyest deejay in the land, DJ Ill Mama. From us to you, keep dreamin', keep believin', and to the other young people in the house, keep your eyes on the prize. Thank you, Chuck Davis! Peace out!" Tre and Mamie grabbed hands and dashed off the stage to meet up with us. I just wanted to get out of there as quickly as possible, but of course they wanted to sign autographs. There was no time to prepare for the hell I was about to catch from my pops.

While Mamie and Tre celebrated a successful show, my father berated me and Collin in the back of the auditorium.

"Damn it, Blue, I'm furious! You lied! Did you really think I wouldn't have been invited to an event like this? I told you that all this nonsense was over. What do you have to say for yourself?" he shouted.

"Dad, I can explain," I pleaded.

"No, forget your explanation. You'll just tell another lie. I will deal with you at home! Get your stuff, and, Collin, take him home right now! Wait until I tell your dad that you were in on this!" he said, storming off.

"Dude, we are beyond busted," Collin said fearfully.

"My life is a wrap," I said, shaking my head.

We gave a round of quick good-byes. Mamie and Tre were confused, but I didn't have time to explain.

We made a mad dash for Collin's car, but he was stopped in his tracks when his phone buzzed with a text from Whiteboy.

"What's wrong?" I asked.

"Check this out. Whiteboy must've sent me a message during the show," he said, clearing his throat. "He wrote 'Sorry about all the drama I caused, but now I gotta do what I gotta do.' Yo, we need to find him!" Collin said.

"I'm down. This is about saving a friend. Let's do it!" I gave him a nod.

"I'm thinkin' we start with the studio or the pool hall. We have to pass Right Trak to get to the other spot," he said.

"Then let's hit the studio first!"

I had two choices: Get to Whiteboy right away, or go home and face something worse than death. Screw it! I'd have to meet my demise with my dad later. Right now we had to save a friend's life.

"Yo, Blue, Collin, where are you guys going?" Mamie yelled, running out to the parking lot after us. Tre and Miles were right behind her.

"Yo, the party just started," Trey shouted. They caught up with us at the car. "Plus, I got some CDs printed up. We could make a killin'!"

"Look, something's going on with Whiteboy. We gotta go!"

"I think he's gonna do something crazy," Collin added, getting into the driver's side.

"If y'all gotta go, then we do too!" Mamie said, and she, Tre, and Miles hopped into the backseat.

We raced in silence against the clock to Right Trak Studios. The adrenaline was pumping. I think we were so worried about Whiteboy, none of us thought about the danger that could be awaiting us.

"Kill your lights when we turn down the block!" Tre said. "I'm from the place where killers run from. These type of street fools ain't no joke."

"Word! Fools get blasted daily in Long Beach. Just be alert and as soon as you hear something sound like it's poppin' off, duck down," Miles warned. I think Miles and Tre were the only ones who weren't scared. We tried to make Mamie go home, but she wasn't having it.

"There's Whiteboy's car down the block," Collin blurted

out. I was about to text Whiteboy, but all of a sudden we heard voices shouting, coming from the direction of the studio entrance. People started running out of the studio. Lopez ran out and jumped in a Dodge Charger. He revved up the engine and waved out the window for his homeboy to hurry. His homie made an attempt to run but was jumped by two other big dudes who proceeded to give him a serious beat-down.

Pop! Pop! Pop!

Lopez screeched off, made a U-turn, and headed in our direction.

"Duck down!" Tre shouted. We quickly followed his orders.

I peeked back over the dashboard only to catch the lightning streak of Whiteboy's Mustang zoom past in hot pursuit of the Charger.

"Go, go, go!" Tre and Miles shouted.

Lopez's Charger was no match for Whiteboy's Mustang, hot on his trail. We lagged behind in Collin's car but could see all the action unfolding through the DC streets. The entrance for I-295 was ahead. As the Charger zipped in and out of lanes, the Mustang lit his trail up. Lopez jumped on the entrance ramp. Whiteboy whipped and weaved, gaining on him.

In a slick move, Lopez dropped his speed and fell back, cutting behind Whiteboy and ramming into his bumper.

"Oh, God, no!" Mamie screamed. Tre put his arm around her. I kept my eyes intensely focused on the road.

"Dude, construction's ahead!" Collin shouted. A car cut

off my view momentarily, then exited. When both cars were in sight again, I could see Whiteboy was now being chased by Lopez. He rammed his car into the side of Whiteboy's. The Mustang swerved, but Lopez wasn't paying attention and was now zooming into the construction zone. ROAD ENDS the giant orange sign announced. It was too late.

In a surreal flow of events, Whiteboy swerved and skidded to a stop, and Collin slammed the brakes, skidding to a stop in the hazard lane. Lopez's Charger lost control, hit the temporary median, flew into the air, and flipped three times, then burst into a ball of flames.

We all jumped out of the car and raced across the highway to Whiteboy's side, where we stood in shock at the horrific display of fireworks. I was speechless. Whiteboy dropped to his knees.

"That could've been me," he said, shaking his head in disbelief.

"But it wasn't," I said, kneeling next to him.

Mamie slowly pulled out her cell phone. "Yes, operator, there's been an accident." Her voice trailed off as we all stood in shock.

"Let's get outta here," Collin said quietly, patting Whiteboy on his shoulder.

In a night that could've taken all of our lives, we were spared for whatever reason. It was strange but I felt like maybe God was trying to tell us all something. Whatever that message was, what was crystal clear was that our bond was stronger than ever.

On the drive home, I guess I wasn't even as worried about the demise that awaited me, even though my dad was, I'm sure, angrier at me than he'd ever been.

As soon as Collin dropped me off and I walked in the door, my father let loose. "Where the hell have you been! We were about to call the police!" he shouted. "I knew he meant business. "Damn it! Why did you lie, Blue?"

"Dad, first off, I'm sorry. I never felt good about lying, but I felt like I had no choice. Take Howard, for instance," I shouted. "You've been shoving it down my throat! I may have been wrong to lie, but you never listen to me!"

"You're damn right you were wrong!" he shouted back. "I give you an inch and you take a mile, Blue. Outside of grounding you forever and taking away all your freedom, I'm at my wits' end!" he yelled even louder, pacing the living room floor. "And what the hell do you mean, you had no choice? I've given you every opportunity in your life so far to do what you want, Blue. I ask for two things: Be honest, and put all your efforts into doing your best in school. I want the truth right now, Blue!"

"Okay." I swallowed hard. "The truth is I've been sneaking out every weekend to work at Club Heat to pay off the money I owe the owner, Rico Tate, for the club damages." I feigned a pained expression, squinting my eyes and twisting my mouth. "And, um, I took the car to get there. But it looks like Tre and

Mamie might be doing *106 and Park*'s Freestyle Friday battle."

"I'm speechless, Blue," he said, slowly sitting down on the couch with a confused look on his face. "You lied to your mother and me, and you made a fool out of me. I'm beyond angry with you, Blue. I'm disappointed." He looked up at me with cold eyes. He didn't look like my father anymore.

I lowered my head. I was ashamed. "Dad, please . . ."

"Was it worth it? Was it worth destroying the trust your parents have for you? Answer me, son."

The door bell rang, breaking up my dad's rant. When I opened it, Jade was standing there, soaking wet from the rain and trembling, eyes bloodshot.

"I'm sorry, but I didn't have anyone else to go to," she said before breaking down. I took her in my arms and let her cry it all out.

"I found out yesterday. They gave her six months. This is unfair! It's wrong!" she screamed. "When she's gone, I won't have anyone. I'll be alone." She broke down crying again.

"Jade," I said, touching the side of her face. "You'll never be alone. You got me." I pulled her closer. She just needed a strong shoulder right now, nothing else.

"I took my anger out on her about not knowing my father. Then I stormed out," she said, sniffling but more calm.

"Jade, I'm realizing more and more each day just how precious life is. I can't even imagine this happening to one of my parents, so I won't front like I understand, but maybe you need to cut her some slack. And maybe it's okay to open up to people who care about you."

"You know Mamie told me about what happened tonight. I don't know what I would've done if something had happened to you all," she said, her eyes filling up with more tears. I just held her tighter.

"I got you," I whispered.

I took her back to the hospital after that. Her mother understood.

"I'm sorry I was so selfish, Mama," Jade said, embracing her.

I hung out in the waiting room until Jade was ready to go, and then I drove her home.

"You all right?" I asked, walking her to the door.

"Yeah. Listen, thank you, Blue. I know I haven't been the easiest person to deal with."

"Stop, Jade, you don't have to explain. I haven't done a lot of stuff right with us, but I'm trying to now."

"No, listen. I block people out because I don't want to be hurt. Maybe I get that part from my dad. I guess I'll never know. I think I've always wondered. That's a terrible feeling, you know, feeling incomplete. My mother, I know, has always tried to overcompensate for me not having a father around, but it wasn't just about him not being here.

"I mean, I could even deal better if maybe he had been here and just didn't come around anymore. At least I could say I met him. I can't even say that. I wonder if I look like him, if I have any siblings. I want to know now more than ever. She's going and I don't know if I can accept that, but it's the reality." Her eyes filled up with tears again.

"Jade, I don't want to get in your business, but maybe when the timing is better you can talk to your mother about finding your father for real. Have you told Mamie?"

"No, no one knows. I'm not ready for all that yet. Please don't tell Collin either." She wrapped her arms around me. "Blue, I don't want to be alone."

Jade pulled me inside the apartment and I couldn't resist touching her. I placed my mouth over hers and kissed her gently. I felt the heat between our bodies as she ran her hands up and down my chest and back. I felt myself getting hard. She wanted it, but I stopped. I know my boys would tell me I was stupid. It was right there for me to take, but something in my gut told me it wasn't right.

Jade needed me. I carried her to her bedroom and laid her across the bed. I slid behind her and rocked her in my arms until she fell asleep. There was no need to say anything else. I had done what I was supposed to do—be there for her. She didn't need sex. The time wasn't right. I might regret it tomorrow, but I doubt it. She needed love now more than ever, and I had plenty of it for her.

CHAPTER THIRTY

COLLIN

This is what I wished for
Just isn't how I envisioned it
—Eminem, "Careful What You Wish For"

Mamie was standing in my driveway with tears streaming down her face when I pulled up.

"What's wrong, Mamie?" I said, dropping my backpack in the driveway.

"Jade's mom is dying." She began to shake and cry uncontrollably.

After she got it out and told me about Jade's mom's cancer, she calmed down and we walked around to the backyard and sat down on two loungers next to the pool. Mamie put her sunglasses on. I looked up at the sky, feeling the late-afternoon sun on my skin.

"You know death is a funny thing. Once you experience it,

it's like you can handle almost anything that comes your way. I remember when Kyle died, I watched everyone crying and all the sadness in their faces and I didn't understand it. I was younger and I thought him 'going away' meant he was going away for a while, but he'd be back."

"That's funny, I thought my mom would be back too." Mamie sniffed, wiping her eyes again.

"Mamie, how long are you going to keep running?"

"I don't know," she said, looking at me with vacant eyes.

"I'm tired of running, running from the truth. I'm tired of my father running and my mother running. I just want to hear my father say Kyle's name. Anything! You know when that car blew up, I found myself wondering, What if it *had* been me. What would my father do or say then?"

"That's funny, I used to imagine what my father would say if I was in a coma or something and he came to visit me. Would he apologize? Would he talk about my mother and how pretty she was and tell me how much he loved her? Would he tell me he was proud of me? And then I wondered, What if I was famous? What would my father say if he saw my CD in the store or saw me in a video or read about me in *USA Today*? Would he call me then?"

"So you never answered my question," I said in a frank tone.

"Oh, about running? Humph! Maybe it's time I start thinking about that," she said, looking into the sky, wiping her eyes again. "I, um, gotta go." She grabbed her purse and stood up. "I've got some business to handle. First up on the list is checking on Jade, and then seeing my aunt. That's gonna be tough, but I need to apologize to her. She didn't just give me a place to stay, she gave me a home. I think I've gotta start, as she would say, 'being the smart girl that I am.' You can lock the pool house. I'm hoping she hasn't given my room away!" She gave an upbeat half smile.

"Mom?" I swallowed hard. "I think I want to come out to the Hamptons on spring break and hang out with you. Fill you in on my life. Maybe talk about Kyle too."

"I'd like that a lot, Collin. There's so much your father and I walked away from. He acts like Kyle never existed, and I guess I keep pretending he's still here," she said softly into the phone. I could hear her quiet tears.

"Mom, it's cool. Let's just talk about it then." She sounded happy for a change. Happy was something that I thought was lost forever, but today we found it. I told her I loved her and hung up. Finding a breakthrough with my father was next. It was going to take a lot more work than reaching out to my mom had been. That was a scary thought, but our relationship wouldn't be free of turmoil until I did so. My entire relationship with him had been based on fear, but for the first time, I was not afraid.

CAN U MEET ME AT THE ART INSTITUTE OF DC IN AN HOUR? WB

NO PROBLEM . . . LET'S DO THIS! C

I smiled at the irony occurring in all of our lives. Whiteboy was gonna do it. He was actually going to face his biggest fear and enroll in art school. He had finally stopped running. I had challenged Mamie to stop running too. I was feeling like I had reached not necessarily a dead end but the end of my race with fear. I jumped in my car and headed across town to meet Whiteboy.

He was standing in the admissions office lobby when I arrived. His body language was stiff and he was jittery.

"You cool?" I asked.

"Damn, man, just nervous, I guess. You think I'm doing the right thing?" he said, giving me a quick pound.

"Dude, I *know* you're doing the right thing."

"I just wanted you or Blue here with me. You guys understand this paperwork stuff," he said nervously, sitting down. I sat down next to him.

"We're your boys, we got your back till the end."

"I know that for real," he said, pounding his chest with his fist. "I've made a lot of mistakes in my life, but I want to put all that behind."

"We all have things that we need to let go of. I know I do."

"Mr. Tommy James?" a woman called out.

"You ready?" I held out my fist.

"GTB fo life! Let's get this art school stuff poppin'!" He tapped my fist and we headed into the director of admission's office.

CHAPTER THIRTY-ONE

We gonna run this town tonight.
—Jay-Z featuring Rihanna and Kanye West, "Run This Town"

**WE WANT YOUNG TRE AND DJ ILL MAMA
ON FRIDAY'S SHOW HIT ME—JD STONE**

I was in shock when I got JD's text. I quickly forwarded it to the crew.

YOU'RE IN THERE THIS FRIDAY NYC 106 & PARK!

My phone buzzed. Mamie had fired a text back to me.

WE BOUT TO BLOW UP! ILL MAMA BOUT TO KILL 'EM

My phone buzzed again. Tre was chiming in.

LET'S TAKE IT TO THE TOP! YOUNG TRE GET MONEY!

BLUE U DID IT DUDE!—C

GTB 4 LIFE HOLLA BACK—WB

Finally, some good news after a week of everything going to hell, from Whiteboy's brush with death to my dad busting me to the news about Jade's mom, if nothing else, this gave me a glimmer of hope that somehow things were going to work out for all of us. I guess if I could wish for anything, it would be for Jade's mom to beat cancer this time.

But the biggest dilemma was going to be breaking it to the crew that I wouldn't be at *106 & Park*. As good as the news was, everything was terrible between me and my parents. The worst feeling in the world is when your mom or dad doesn't have your back or trust you anymore.

"Blue?" my father said, knocking on my bedroom door and entering. He was holding some papers in his hand. "I checked on your grades. You really are working hard. I knew you had it in you." He sat down next to me.

"I still got a lot of hard work ahead of me." I was still too embarrassed after everything to look him in the eye.

"My buddy Mr. Jones shot me an e-mail saying that in just

these past four or five weeks you've made a tremendous turn-around with your attitude and participation in class. Despite the lying and sneaking out, you're really living up to your potential, Blue, and that's what high school is about. You're going to do fine in life," he said solemnly. "I'm still not over everything, but I'm not as angry as I was. You should thank your mother for that."

"Dad, I know that apologizing isn't enough. Your trust means everything to me. I'm going to show you and earn back your trust."

"I just thought you were smarter than how you've been act-ing. You acted stupidly the other night defying me, and then going after your friend. You could've been in that exploding car. And Whiteboy is lucky. I made some calls and got any charges he could've been facing dropped. I don't know if you realize your own future could've been lost. Your mother and I would've lost our only son, senselessly. It's time to grow up in your think-ing, Blue. Eventually lies catch up with you, and in this life all you have is your word and your reputation."

"Dad, honestly, my real motivation before was Rico Tate's promise to put me down and teach me what I needed to know about the entertainment game, but that was then . . ." I took a deep breath.

"How much money do you still owe that guy?" he said with a tight expression.

"Looks like that debt is settled, but I'm going to look for a job to pay back the five hundred I took from my college money. And I'm going to work hard to get into Howard."

"I don't want you to go to Howard for me, Blue. I want you to go because you want to."

"It's what I want," I said with conviction.

"Blue," he said, standing up. "I realize I can't put you in a box to be exactly who I want you to be. I can't hold you down, that would be wrong. A good parent provides the guardrails in life at a certain point. I think we're at that point. I'm not going to allow you to fail, but I'm also not going to make you throw away *your* dreams." My father's words meant more than any amount of money or gift he could buy. His support, his endorsement, it was priceless.

YO NEED A FAVOR . . . PLS REPRESENT FOR ME AT 106 & PARK

I sent Collin a text five minutes ago, but he still hadn't responded. I was about to tell him to forget it when my Sidekick buzzed:

DUDE . . . YOU GOT IT!

I smiled to myself. My boy had my back for sure and maybe it was best to put a pin in things for now. The one thing I admired about Collin was that making his father proud was a priority for him. Maybe that wasn't so bad. Who knows? Maybe once I graduated from Howard University, my dad would be my first investor!

It was Friday and I was trying not to think about the whole *106 & Park* thing. I had made myself okay with not going with everybody. Even though Collin wasn't down with getting back with Blue Up, he was definitely lookin' out. I knew he'd represent me well.

"Blue, someone's here to see you!" my mother called out. When I walked down the steps, my solemn expression quickly spread to a smile. My mom and dad had gathered my entire crew in our living room.

"What took you so long?" Collin announced.

"Now, you know I couldn't light 'em up without you!" Tre said.

"Yeah, we're about to take the crown, baby!" Mamie added. When I saw Jade standing behind her, my face lit up. Everything in the room momentarily stopped. She walked over and wrapped her arms around me. "My mom says good luck!"

"You rollin' too?" I said.

"My mom said I needed to go and be with my friends. So I took her advice. She'll be watching from the hospital." I gave her another big hug before running upstairs to grab an overnight bag.

When I came back downstairs, I turned to my dad with a big smile.

"Sometimes parents have to be adult enough to admit when we're wrong too." My dad smiled back. "Son, we may not see eye-to-eye on everything, but I recognize that you've got a dream, and I realize that as your dad I can either help you make that dream happen, or push you away and that dream may go away. I don't want to push you away." I walked up to my dad and gave him a pound and then a hug. He pulled away and checked his watch. "New York is about a four-hour drive, isn't it?"

"No, Mr. Reynolds, three when I'm driving!" Collin said, holding up the keys.

"That's what I'm talkin' 'bout!" Whiteboy added, giving him a pound. We all broke into laughter.

I watched the world whizzing by as we sped down I-95 and onto the New Jersey Turnpike. I put my arm around Jade. She rested her head on my shoulder. I saw Tre do the same with Mamie. Miles slid their mix into the CD player, and Collin turned up the volume and slipped on his sunglasses. Whiteboy was pretty chilled, just staring out the window.

The bangin' track had all of us bobbing our heads. I closed my eyes, thankful that even with all the ups and downs, I had times like this to remind me not only of how precious life is but of how much talent me and my crew had. All you need sometimes is that crack in the door. Then you can kick it wide open.

About the Author

Lyah Beth LeFlore, television producer and author, is one of today's most talented and respected creative forces. She's been featured in the *New York Times*, *Essence* magazine, *Ebony*, *Jet*, and *Entertainment Weekly*; also on CNN and BET. Television producer credits include: *New York Undercover* (FOX), *Midnight Mac* starring Bernie Mac (HBO), and *Grown Ups* (UPN). Her books include the coauthored *Cosmopolitan Girls*; the Essence bestseller *Last Night a DJ Saved My Life*; and the *New York Times* bestseller and *Essence* bestseller *I Got Your Back: A Father and Son Keep It Real About Love, Fatherhood, Family, and Friendship*—the nonfiction collaboration with Grammy Award father and son Eddie and Gerald Levert. *I Got Your Back* was a 2008 nominee/finalist for the *Essence* Literary Awards and the NAACP Image Awards. In 2008 Lyah also wrote the CD liner notes for The O'Jays' *The Essential O'Jays* and for multi-platinum artist Usher's *Here I Stand*. Lyah's third novel, *Wildflowers* (Broadway Books/Crown Publishing Group), arrives fall 2009. And now, with the hot new teen series The Come Up, she's expanding her fan base to include teen readers. Lyah, thirty-eight, is a native of St. Louis, Missouri, and holds a BA in Communications Media from Stephens College. In May 2005 she became the youngest member of the Stephens College Board of Trustees, and only the second African American to be appointed to the board in the college's history. She is also a member of the Alpha Kappa Alpha Sorority Incorporated. For more info go to lyahbethleflore.com.

About the Illustrator

DL Warfield is among the most consistent creative minds in visual branding, design, product and content development, youth culture, advertising, and marketing. His reputation has evolved from artistic mastermind to celebrated idea leader. He is a native of St. Louis, Missouri, and a graduate of Washington University's School of Fine Arts. He started his career as a product developer and creative consultant for the fashion retail corporation Edison Brothers Stores, Inc., creating logos and clothing designs for their super-successful Oaktree, Shifty's, and Factory brand divisions. Before long, Tommy Boy Records came calling, resulting in his acceptance of the title of head designer of the powerful record label's clothing line. Following an exciting tenure at Tommy Boy, DL became the resident art director at LaFace Records in Atlanta, Georgia. At LaFace, DL worked with some of today's hottest recording artists: Usher, TLC, OutKast, and Pink. He also received critical acclaim for designing the album artwork for OutKast's 1996 LP, *ATLiens*, as well as TLC's final album, *FanMail*. After LaFace shut its doors in 2000, DL launched his own company, GOLDFINGER c.s. Since its inception, clients include Nike, Sprite, Heineken, Anheuser-Busch, Geffen Records, Sony Latin Entertainment, DreamWorks Records, Sony Music, OutKast Inc., Universal Records, Nordstrom, Ryan-Kenny Clothing Company, Arista Records, HBO, Virgin Records, Coca-Cola, Adidas, *Vibe*, GMC, and Song Airlines, to name a few. DL won the Bacardi Liquor "Cultural Architect" award in 2002; he was a finalist in the Hennessy Black Masters 2007 Art Competition; and in 2004 and 2005, DL was the winner of the Timberland Community Outreach Program, and commissioned to design a signature boot and mural in Atlanta for Timberland. As he continues to support various community awareness programs, his passion to diversify has only intensified, and the "creative crusader" is now intent on building cultural, social, and creative bridges.

Simon & Schuster's **Simon Teen**
e-newsletter delivers current updates on
the hottest titles, exciting sweepstakes, and
exclusive content from your favorite authors.

Visit **TEEN.SimonandSchuster.com** to
sign up, post your thoughts, and find out what
every avid reader is talking about!